CAMP CARNAGE

A

NIGHT TERRORS

Novel

Elliot Arthur Cross & Joshua Winning

MMXIV

A very special thanks to our beta readers

● ● ●

Book layout by Elliot Arthur Cross.

Cover design by John Brock.

Old log cabin wood wall background © Mona Makela | Dreamstime.com.

ISBN 978-1500694234

Printed in the United States of America

First printing, August 2014

Contents

Prologue

August 2, 1983

The summer heat had eased off and Miles took a grateful breath of the cool evening air. Back in Dallas, his hometown, the sidewalks practically sizzled all year round, but even he'd found the sweltering Colorado weather tough this week. He was glad that being a camper at Camp Genesis meant he got to wear shorts and a vest and goof off in the lake most of the time; otherwise he'd have melted into a gooey monster version of himself days ago. Hell, it was so hot he'd have worn nothing if he could get away with it. For some reason, though, the counselors frowned on nudity.

"Gorgeous, huh?" he sighed. As much as he hated the anti-gay activities they were forced to endure there, he couldn't deny the camp's beauty.

"What?"

Beside him, Blake looked blank and Miles shot him a glare. Blake didn't appreciate the peace of the dusky woods like Miles did. He came from Kentucky, where every sunset was a living postcard. He was taller, barely seventeen, and his tanned, defined arms gleamed blue in the moonlight. Miles shoved him, but Blake's innocent smile made being angry so goddamn difficult.

Grinning mischievously, Miles tore off into the woods.

"Catch me if you can!"

"Hey!" Blake called, but Miles ignored him. He liked being chased. Maybe it was some sort of residual caveman mentality. Or was it cavemen who did the chasing? He couldn't think clearly over the hammering of his heart. Perhaps it was cave*women* who liked being chased? Either way, he was soon panting and shimmering with sweat. He had to slow down, but he didn't care.

Getting caught was the fun part.

It didn't take Blake long to catch up. Strong hands seized Miles' bare shoulders and he laughed, tossing back a head of sandy blond curls. His back hit a tree trunk, knocking the breath out of him, but then there was Blake, bringing their lips together. He tasted like cherry pie and chewing gum.

"It's my lunch money, isn't it?" Miles gasped melodramatically. "Just take it, please. Don't whale on me."

Blake looked confused for a moment. His brown puppy-dog eyes widened—sweet, simple Blake, so very much the product of his farm upbringing—but then he grinned and bit his lip. He pressed into Miles, his body heat divine torture.

"Yeah," he said. "I really like, uh, sloppy joes, and…tater tots."

Miles laughed again. A bird flapped over their heads, disappearing into the canopy, which let in thin shafts of silver light.

They both froze.

"Miles, what if somebody catches us out here?"

He grabbed Blake's ass in both hands.

"They'll have to ask my permission to spank you, because this is all mine."

"Seriously, Miles, we could get in deep shit."

For a guy as big and powerful as Blake, he sure was a pussy sometimes. Miles liked that, though. He didn't get to play the strong one often.

"Come on." He took Blake's hand and pulled him through the woods.

"Where—" Blake began, but Miles held a finger to his lips. "Shhhh."

2

They made their way between the trees, fingers entwined, finally emerging into the moonlight. The lake was still, like liquid mercury, and a boathouse rested at its edge.

More of a shack than a house. It was that old and decrepit and Miles felt confident nobody would disturb them there.

"The boathouse?" Blake murmured, uncertainty in his voice. "Isn't it condemned or something?"

"What can I say? I've always wanted to act out *The Love Boat* for real."

Miles turned the dial on the rusted padlock.

"You know the code?" Blake cast worried looks about them, puppy-dog eyes wider than ever. Miles couldn't help thinking it was adorable—and oh so ironic. *Miles the bad boy.* His mother would have a fit if she knew he'd snuck out there with another guy while the rest of the camp slept.

Good.

He was in half a mind to tell her every sordid detail, just to see the expression on her face. *That'd* make her take notice, stop harping on about her own miserable mother. Serve her right for enlisting him at this ridiculous camp. It was meant to fix him. Straighten him out, so to speak. Make him a real man.

Real my ass.

"There," he said, brandishing the padlock triumphantly. "Just call me Magnum, PI."

The door creaked loudly and Miles flinched, ushering Blake inside quickly before pulling it shut behind them.

Miles would have been creeped out inside the boathouse if Blake wasn't with him. A lone paddling boat rested half-submerged in the water, slowly rotting like a slumbering sailor. Cobwebs looped across the ceiling and junk cluttered every corner. Rusty tools hung on racks and Miles thought he saw a mouse skitter away. At least he hoped it was a mouse.

"See? Romantic as hell," he said with a grin.

3

"This place gives me the creeps."

"Don't be such a baby."

"Want to take my mind off it?" Blake sheepishly shoved a hand through his floppy black hair.

"Grrrrr!" Miles snarled, pawing at Blake's chest.

He loved what Blake did to him. Miles had never been so forward in his life. Back in Dallas, he'd never have dreamt of talking to a guy like Blake. He'd dreaded coming to the camp again. Even in the picturesque surroundings, the previous years had been miserable. But not anymore. This year he had Blake.

He hadn't believed it when Blake showed up all athletic and naïve. Miles had watched him from afar for a few weeks, admiring the view as the jock strolled around Camp Genesis, blissfully unaware of the way everybody drooled over him. They'd barely said twenty words to each other when Miles received the news that changed everything. His dad was dead. Suicide. It came out of nowhere. Miles' dad was the kind of guy who always looked on the bright side. Miles couldn't imagine him taking his own life, but it made sense looking back on it. You'd have to be unhinged to marry the type of woman his father had.

In the wake of the news, Miles fell apart. He was only allowed a day off camp for the funeral, and when he got back, the other campers treated him like a leper; like something bad would happen to their loved ones by association.

Blake was different. One day, he stayed behind to make sure Miles was okay while the others had a swimming lesson. He'd sat on Miles' bed and listened while Miles rambled on in between sobs. Blake had pulled him in for a hug, and as they held each other, Miles realized Blake had a boner…

What started out as a comforting make-out session quickly developed into a real relationship. That was three weeks ago, and Blake had helped Miles whenever he retreated into himself. They had to be discreet about their relationship, stealing kisses in the dark and passing notes during mealtimes, but that made it all the more thrilling.

In the dark of the boathouse, Miles pulled Blake closer, pressing his mouth against Blake's sun-chapped lips, savoring the way he tasted. He smelled like a man, sweaty and alluring.

It was a miracle. Somebody this sweet returning Miles' affection. And a guy, even. He'd had to avoid awkward flirtations from girls for a few years, but now he felt like the awkward one making passes. Besides a few old perverts around Dallas, Blake was a first. And it wasn't just because Blake felt sorry for him— no one could fake a boner like that with a snotty, puffy-eyed guy during a crying jag. He seemed to genuinely care. Everything was so easy for him. He didn't seem that fazed at attending such a bizarre camp; he even put up with the stupid rehabilitation exercises without complaining.

Blake jerked away. "What was that?"

"I didn't hear anything."

"I heard something."

"Maybe it's the creature from the Black Lagoon," Miles teased.

"Black Lagoon?"

Miles sighed and wrapped his arms around Blake's shoulders.

"Just forget it," Miles said, giving him a reassuring kiss.

Then he heard it, too. A weird popping sound. His grip on Blake slackened and he looked around for the source of the noise. His gaze rested on the inky water. Bubbles burst on the otherwise still surface. Miles jumped back, half expecting a nest of giant water snakes to explode out of the water at them, but then the water settled again.

"What the hell—" Miles began.

A shadowy figure erupted from the water. Before either of them could react, something shiny flashed in the dark and Blake made a guttural choke. Warmth spattered Miles' face and he stared at Blake, mouth wide in shock.

Blood gushed from Blake's mouth. He choked, confusion twisting his pretty face.

Something was wrong with his neck. Something protruded from it. Something sharp and dripping blood.

"M-M-M—" Blake reached out for Miles as he collapsed to the floor.

The dark figure turned, obscured by deep shadows.

"What's going on?" Miles demanded.

He couldn't think of anything else to say. He wouldn't have to think of anything else.

Something flashed in the dark once more.

Garden shears, Miles realized as they sank into his skull.

Chapter 1

July 16, 1986

Billy Collins rested his forehead against the car window, enjoying the vibrations that traveled through him. Anything to distract him from where he was going. His *Masters of the Universe* game console rested in his lap; the batteries had died already. He had more somewhere, probably in his bag in the trunk.

If he was He-Man, he wouldn't have had to catch a plane and then suffer the stale-smelling rental car just to reach his own personal vacation to Hell.

"This place is going to suck," he muttered.

"Hmmm?"

Beside him, his father squeezed the steering wheel with his hands at a perfect "ten and two." A model citizen. It must have killed him that his son was gay. How could it possibly happen to a guy like Ted Collins? Decorated pediatrician, graduate of New York Medical College, married with kids, still had all his hair at forty-five—and not a one gray. His life would have been perfect if it wasn't for his son, who'd decided he liked chasing pants instead of skirts.

"I don't get why I have to go." Billy didn't complain often; he'd been raised well. A real city boy, unfazed by most things. Even at seventeen he'd never thrown a teenage tantrum. But being forced into camp pushed him to his limit. "It blows."

"Language," his father said evenly. "We've discussed this, William. It's for the best."

"*You* discussed it with *Mom*. I wasn't part of any discussion."

He remembered the first time he'd heard about Camp Genesis. He'd been eavesdropping on his parents through the kitchen door, late enough that they thought he was in bed. They'd been acting strangely all week, ever since his little brother Jake had found Billy's only gay magazine hidden under his mattress. He'd felt guilty for weeks after buying the magazine and was half relieved when it came out in the open. Billy had known something wasn't right, so he snuck downstairs and held his breath as he listened to his mom and dad discussing sending him away. His pulse raced faster and faster. They were so calm about it, talking about Camp Genesis the way they did when they were preparing for surgery.

They didn't mention the camp to him the next morning. Or the morning after that. A tense week followed before they finally brought it up. Billy had begged and pleaded with them, but their minds were made up. He'd spent the entire week praying they would change their minds, but he had never been that lucky.

"Now, William—" His father paused, brightening. "Ah, here we are!"

Billy hated it when he used his full name. He pulled back from the window. A makeshift sign at the side of the road read CAMP GENESIS. An arrow next to a leaning mailbox pointed down a dirt road. Billy wished he had He-Man's sword to slash the sign in half. As they turned onto the side road, Billy's stomach flipped sickeningly. *This is it. All roads lead to Hell.*

They trundled down the winding track until they reached the entrance to the camp. The Camp Genesis name ran across an arch over the road. The letters on the weathered wood looked faded and forbidding.

Billy took a breath as they drove beneath it. He couldn't remember the last time he'd cried, but faced with this humiliation, he felt like screaming, shouting or weeping. He bit his lip. If he had to go to this jail, he'd go with dignity.

"What a crock," he muttered.

A camp for gay kids. No, a camp against *gay kids.*

He'd never heard of anything so ridiculous. How the hell did these people expect to "rehabilitate" him? Shove him in a football jersey and force him to make out with girls? Just the thought made him queasy. And besides, wasn't stranding a load of gay kids in an isolated camp the stupidest idea ever? It was like leading a starving man to a banquet and telling him not to eat.

"Looks pretty 'rad' to me," his father joked as they pulled into a clearing.

Billy rolled his eyes but scrutinized the camp out of morbid curiosity. A number of wooden huts were grouped around a main building. A lake glimmered in the distance, framed by tall trees. It looked quaint, like it hadn't been updated since the '50s. He wondered if they even had electricity and running water this far away from civilization. Kids were everywhere. Some crying and clinging to their parents, others leaning against trees and puffing smoke. They seemed to range from around fifteen to eighteen in age. How could he fit in there? A scrawny city boy. He definitely wasn't one of the cool kids.

Nerd.

His father pulled the car to a stop and got out.

Begrudgingly, Billy popped open his door and stepped into the summer heat. He wished he hadn't worn jeans and a *Star Wars* T-shirt featuring C-3PO, his favorite character. It was hotter than in New York. A dry, airless Colorado heat that he'd only ever experienced when he went to Arizona on vacation with his folks.

Something hit Billy in the back and he stumbled, grabbing the car door.

"Hey, sorry man!"

He straightened up and was met with a million-dollar smile. The other guy looked Billy's age, but he was tall and muscular.

9

He swept his floppy brown hair out of his dazzling blue eyes. Billy couldn't breathe.

The other guy clutched a football. Why were all the hot guys jocks?

"My bad," the guy said. "Catch ya later." His sneakers flashed red as he raced off to hurl the ball at another guy. Somebody like that couldn't be gay, could he? Most of the guys Billy had seen on the streets of New York were femme or wore lots of leather. Maybe this guy was a junior counselor or a cook. He waved to someone else and then disappeared behind one of the cabins.

"Here."

Billy snapped out of it and took his bags from his father, who gave him a disapproving look that bordered on genuine concern.

"You be good," his father said, clearly attempting to convey more than just those three words. "I'll see you in a couple of weeks. Your mom will send cookies."

Store-bought.

"Okay."

Billy nodded and his father ruffled his straight black hair—it was so affectionate and rare that Billy was almost surprised to tears. "We'll miss you, kiddo."

His father got back in the car and drove away, leaving Billy alone with the blinding sunshine and the sound of screaming in his ears. He watched his dad's rental car as it slowly followed a jeep under the Camp Genesis sign and out of view down the winding path.

Billy stood, dazed, in the clearing at the front of the camp, a death grip on his bags. He couldn't build up enough courage to head toward the main building and he half considered turning around and making for the exit, hitchhiking back to New York. Then somebody started talking to him.

"You look like you could use a drink."

"Huh?"

"I'm Jem, short for Jemima, but if you tell anybody that I'll feed you to my dog."

The girl beside him was slightly taller, around the same age as him, her shoulder-length hair a savage shade of purple. She wore hoop earrings, a baggy pink vest top and stretch pants with stirrups. Billy thought she looked like she'd stepped out of a Cyndi Lauper video—his friend had her album, *Blue Angel*—but there was a toughness to Jem that meant she carried the extreme fashion easily. She held a duffel bag in one hand and a green backpack was slung over her shoulder.

"Er, hi, I'm Billy," he said, dropping one bag and putting his hand out stiffly.

"Looks like you came to the wrong camp—the nerd rehab's down the road."

"How do you know I'm a nerd?" Billy asked. She just smiled and pointed at his T-shirt. "Right, 3PO."

Idiot. Why was he acting like a forty-year-old? *Be cool.*

"I, er—"

She broke into laughter.

"Just messing with you. Sheesh, this place screwing with your head already, huh? It's a genuine shit-hole."

She pronounced it *gen-you-ine.*

Billy grinned. Any enemy of Camp Genesis was a friend of his. He hoped.

"It's my first time at camp," he admitted.

"Mine, too. I say we burn it down now and head for the hills. Gotta be better than sticking around these homophobes."

"I have matches," Billy said.

Jem wrapped an arm around his shoulder. "You and me Bill, we're gonna get along just fine."

"Billy," he corrected her before he could stop himself.

"Come on, let's go to registration. They'll probably brand our feet in case we hop the fences, but it'll only hurt a couple of days. *God*, there better be cute girls here."

• • •

From the shade of a lone oak tree, a figure watched the kids as they arrived. Unseen and unnoticed by all of them, he squinted and pouted miserably.

Look at 'em all, horsing around without a damn care in the world.

"You're all gonna die…"

A hoarse whisper rattled contempt at the bratty kids. His leg itched and he could hardly wait to return to his shack for another drink.

"You're all gonna die…"

Chapter 2

The main building looked like something out of *The Parent Trap*. Billy had seen it at a downtown New York theater during a musical revival season. He'd gone with his parents and Jack, his five-year-old brother. Jack had loved it; Billy had rolled his eyes a lot.

Something told him nobody would break into song like Hayley Mills here, though. He wondered if he'd meet his identical twin and have a Disney adventure. That almost sounded as bad as the camp's anti-gay program. He wasn't sure what activities they had planned for them, but he feared the worst. What if they hooked him up to electrodes and tried to shock the gay out of him?

"It's worse than I thought." Jem grimaced next to him. "And I don't see any hot chicks, yet."

The smell of bleach mingled with old wood in the main hall. A stage rested down the back, over which hung a banner: *WELCOME CAMPERS — Smile and the world smiles with you.*

"Barf and the world barfs with you," Jem muttered.

Rows of chairs faced the stage and a few bored-looking kids were already lounging in them. One girl did her make-up and another kid stuck his gum under his seat.

Billy's insides rattled. They'd checked in just outside at a folding table and been instructed to go in and find a seat. The counselor who registered them seemed cheerful. Almost too cheerful, Billy thought, and she looked barely older than him.

"Back row?" Jem asked.

"No funny business."

"Scout's honor."

They sat in the back and watched as the hall filled up. Billy felt his cheeks get hotter when the brunet guy who'd bumped into him took a seat a few rows ahead of them. Suddenly conscious of how he looked, Billy tugged at his dark hair, which was parted into curtains. He must look a mess after the long car ride. This wasn't going to be easy.

With a start, he realized somebody had appeared next to him. The newcomer had sat down so quietly it was like a ghost had materialized out of thin air. The new kid was like a mouse in human form; even skinnier than Billy, and only about fifteen, a long brown fringe falling into his light green eyes. Dressed in a bright T-shirt and shorts that made him look even younger, he seemed to be hoping the ground would open beneath him and swallow him whole.

"Hi," Billy said, deciding he couldn't have too many friends in a place like this.

The other boy blushed a violent crimson.

"I'm Billy, and that's Jem."

"Peace." Jem saluted him.

"Tommy," the other boy said. He even sounded like a mouse.

"You know anybody here?" Billy asked. He couldn't help feeling sorry for the guy; the look of misery plastered across Tommy's face was awful.

Tommy shook his head, his hair swishing like a mop.

"Hey, we're all sisters here." Jem shrugged at him. "United we stand against the evil that is summer camp."

Tommy cracked a surprisingly cute smile and Billy was glad he'd bumped into Jem outside. She was just what the camp needed—the only way to fight idiots like these was with a sense of humor.

When every chair was filled—he guessed there were about thirty—a stern-looking woman strolled on stage. She looked smart in a blouse and pencil skirt, sort of resembling the business types Billy saw on the subway. There was something almost masculine about her, though. Her jaw was granite, her posture arrogant. If the heat was getting to her, she didn't show it; if anything, an icy draft came off her like she'd been in the deep freezer all summer. Billy pitied the kids in the front row.

"Welcome to Camp Genesis," the woman said in a clipped tone that caused a hush to settle over the hall. "I'm Katherine Creevey, the camp director, and I'm very pleased to have you all here."

"Doesn't sound it," Jem whispered.

"Yeah," Billy whispered back.

"You're here because you need our help," Katherine continued piously. "You're here for correctional treatment at the behest of your parents. Their concerns are our concerns. By the time you leave here in six weeks, you'll all be fully-rounded adults armed with the tools you need to face the challenges of the world and the temptations of the Devil."

Growing bored already, Billy noticed the quiet man standing at her side. A priest, if his outfit was anything to go by. He looked about sixty and he surveyed the audience with a look of compassion. Billy thought he must have been sweating to death all in black, but he didn't look uncomfortable in the slightest.

"The Genesis program is structured to give you a new life, just as God breathed life into Adam and Eve."

"I thought it was Adam and Steve," a goofy-looking kid said. A few of the campers chuckled, until Katherine shot them icy stares. Billy imagined lasers shooting from her eyes.

"I don't take my responsibility lightly," Katherine continued briskly, a slight Southern twang to her voice. Billy wondered if she was from Texas. *Figures.* "And I expect you all to take your time here seriously. This is not a holiday. You'll meet your cabin leaders soon and you'll treat them all with the utmost respect." She paused, looking from face to face. "If you are discovered to be breaking the rules in any way, all privileges will be immediately removed. Any form of fraternizing is strictly forbidden."

As she glared at her audience, Billy couldn't help imagining her with a Swastika on her blouse and a moustache over her top lip. To his surprise, Katherine's gaze bore momentarily into him and he felt his throat reddening. He stiffened in his seat.

"Now," Katherine said. "I'd also like to introduce Father Oliver, whom you'll all meet in due course to discuss your areas of concern. Father Oliver."

The man at her side cleared his throat and beamed, his cheeks glowing rosily.

"Welcome," he greeted them, spreading his arms as if he wanted to embrace them all. "You are most welcome here, truly."

"Who let Santa Claus in?" Jem hissed. Billy bit his lip to keep from laughing. Though the priest was clean-shaven and thin, his salt and pepper hair gave him a Christmassy air—paired with his jolly manner, it really was like having a skinny Saint Nick in the room.

"What a fine bunch of bananas," the priest continued. "I look forward to meeting you all individually. Camp Genesis is your home for the next six weeks, so please treat it as such. The other counselors have been hard at work concocting fun activities for you all. You're in for a real treat."

Billy couldn't help liking him. He seemed genuine, like a proud grandfather, whereas Katherine Creevey was as appealing as an icicle.

"I'd like to start as we mean to go on," Father Oliver said. "Please join me in the Lord's Prayer. *Our Father, which art in Heaven...*"

Billy mumbled along with the other kids, though he barely knew the words. He was pretty sure the goofy-looking kid a few rows up was reciting a version Father Oliver would disapprove of. He wouldn't last long here.

Through it all, Katherine watched, her robotic manner unsettling.

"Now, I think I've jabbered on enough," Father Oliver said finally. "During registration you were all assigned a cabin number. I think it's time you all got settled in. And no fighting over bunks, eh? There are plenty to go around."

As the kids in the hall started bustling from their seats, Katherine's voice rang over them.

"In an orderly fashion! We're not animals, are we?"

"Only in the sack," a guy in front of Billy said. Katherine didn't seem to hear, but the entire row burst into giggles. She eyed them suspiciously but remained silent, her hands clasped before her.

As he prepared to leave the hall, Billy noticed a man at the back staring at him. Dishevelled in a stain-splattered shirt, dark bags under his eyes, the man fixed him a look that he couldn't decipher.

"Hey," Billy said to Jem. "Who's that guy?"

"No idea. Local bum?"

A crowd of kids blocked the man from view and when Billy got to the door, he'd vanished.

"Well, catch ya later, Bill," Jem said, punching him on the arm. "I'm off to Cabin Two. Tommy, try not to break any hearts on the way to your bunk."

She was already ambling away when Billy realized Tommy had followed them out and was hovering nervously next to him. He felt a slight twinge, recalling how his brother, Jack, often did the same thing.

"Don't hit the showers without me," Billy called back at Jem, surprising himself. There was something about Jem that made him feel at ease. "And...it's Billy." She'd already flipped him the peace sign and turned her back.

"Which cabin are you in?" he asked Tommy.

"Um, number four."

"Cool. Same here."

Cabin Four, where are you? As he surveyed the community of wooden huts, he noticed a shadow skirting the edge of the woods. He frowned and squinted. It was the dishevelled man from the hall. He stumbled over something, grunted and disappeared between the trees.

Chapter 3

Kyle Majors was pissed at himself. Growing up with three older brothers, he knew you had to act quickly and aggressively if you wanted something. At the Majors' house, only children who elbowed their way to the center of the table got garlic bread or apple pie. He'd been too damn slow and now this Billy kid got to share bunk beds with Neal, the cute blue-eyed Adonis with the killer arms.

Trying to hide his sneer, Kyle tossed his bag on the one free bed. He glanced up at the average-looking guy sitting on the top bunk, pasty legs swinging back and forth. He'd only noticed him before because he made the Adam and Steve comment during Katherine's power spiel.

"Hey, I'm Brady." He had dark hair and a lopsided grin.

"Kyle." He couldn't hide his disgust as Brady munched on chips, the plastic bag crunching loudly.

He couldn't believe he was back here again. A second year at Camp Genesis. Last year, he'd slept in a different cabin and shared a bunk with an adorable Christian boy. He'd managed two summer flings with a couple of naïve boys. Ever since his parents told him they were sending him back, he'd fantasized about some sexy guy sleeping right above him, but Brady wasn't exactly the stuff of wet dreams. Kyle had quickly realized he was the only returning camper, and the hottest guy there, besides himself, was Neal.

He probably plays football. Wonder if he got caught receiving in his tight end.

"Okay, everyone," their counselor announced. "I want you guys to get your things put away so we don't have all these bags cluttering up the place. Then we'll get to know each other and go over the bunk's rules. All right?"

"You got it," Billy said.

Brown-nosing skinny nerd.

Kyle surveyed Billy, the black hair hanging like curtains on his face, his shorter frame, and his scrawny build. He was clearly no competition for Neal's affection.

As Kyle unpacked his clothes, he eyed Neal's tall, muscular body and vowed he'd score by the end of camp.

A chubby kid huffed and puffed as he put his things away and a skinny black boy whistled as he worked.

Once everyone was settled in, the stocky counselor carried a chair from his adjoining room and set it in the doorway. The eight boys sat on their bunks, all waiting for him to do something.

"Let's get started. My name's Glen," the counselor said. He wore thick, Coke-bottle glasses and tapped one foot against the floorboards as he talked. "A little about me. I'm from the lakes region of Michigan, which could describe all of Michigan." He chuckled. No one else did. "I got involved with Camp Genesis through my church and I thought it would be a great way to help people and get some sunshine during the summer. Having a lake and working on my tan sure beats ladling out soup to the homeless, am I right? Why don't you guys introduce yourselves?" He pointed to the pudgy boy on the bottom of the corner bunk.

"Uh, I'm Cobb," he said shyly.

"Like, as in corn on the?" Kyle asked with a grin.

"I guess so," Cobb said. He looked like he ate plenty of corn, plus anything else he saw. "I got in trouble last year at fat camp. With another guy." Kyle shuddered at the mental image. "I lost twelve pounds but I found them again after getting back home."

"Okay, great, let's keep it going." Counselor Glen nodded encouragement at the guy sitting on the bunk above Cobb. Kyle hadn't even noticed he was there.

"I'm Tommy." Kyle had to strain to hear him. "I, uh, I don't know why I'm here. It's a mistake."

Sure it is, sweetie.

Kyle vaguely remembered seeing Tommy talking with Billy at registration, which made him enemy number two.

"I'm Billy, and I'm from New York City. I, um, haven't done anything with anyone before."

"Big surprise," Kyle muttered. He realized he'd said it out loud when everyone turned their heads toward him, and quickly followed it up with, "Surprising, you seem like a nice guy." He rolled his eyes and looked up at Neal.

"I'm Neal, and I wouldn't even have to be here, but I only live about ten minutes away. I'm not queer or anything, my parents are just confused."

Yeah, they're *the ones who are confused.*

Kyle imagined what it would take to convince Neal that he really did like guys. It would probably involve skinny-dipping in the lake and a little trick Kyle liked to call "the blowtorch." That ought to do it.

"I'm Steven, and I'm from Pennsylvania," said a preppy-looking black guy with a lisp, snapping Kyle from his daydream. He figured Steven was lucky he wasn't from Mississippi, otherwise the lisp would really get him in trouble. He sat on the bottom bunk next to Kyle's, his hands folded neatly in his lap. "I don't know if I'm gay or not, but my dad is super worried."

"Don't worry, buddy," Glen said. "When you get back home, he'll have nothing to worry about. Who's next?"

"I'm Matthew," an intense-looking short guy said. "I live with my grandmother who disapproves of everything anyone does anywhere. She wanted the summer to herself, so here I am."

Kyle realized it was his turn. He rolled his eyes again.

"Kyle Majors. This is my second summer at Camp Genesis. I guess my cure didn't take last year so Katherine offered my parents a discount to give it another whirl. Their loss."

"What do you mean it didn't take?" Brady asked with an incredulous chuckle. "Like what, you got caught fooling around with a senior?"

"Two of them," Kyle said, smirking at the memory. He shot Billy a look.

Yeah, buddy, I got moves. Don't mess with me.

Brady received an expectant look from their counselor and hastily said, "Oh, I'm Brady. Coming here was kind of a last minute thing. My folks freaked out when they caught me smoking pot. They wanted to send me to rehab, but they couldn't afford it. Then they found out I was seeing my neighbor, Stanley. I don't think they're that upset that I'm gay, they just figured this was a cheaper alternative, 'cause there's no way I'm going to smoke pot while I'm here, wink wink."

"That's just great, everybody," Glen said. His sunny optimism made Kyle want to punch him.

Happy pills. Has to be.

"I'm sure we'll get to know each other a lot better and be great friends," the counselor continued. "You know, it's perfectly fine if you haven't messed around with anyone. I'm a virgin, and proud of it. God wants us to wait until our wedding day. Consider yourself at an advantage, Billy." The virgin blushed and leaned back into the shadows of his bed. "I want to get something clear, right off the bat. The other boys' cabin has younger campers, and since you guys are a little older, I don't want to have to babysit you every minute of the day. Now I'll be sleeping right in that room. The walls are thin, and I won't tolerate any fooling around. I don't mean camp jokes and pranks like a water bucket over a door, so long as it's not *my* door. What I mean is anything *gay*.

We're here to have fun and get you guys cured."

"There's nothing to cure," said Matthew, the tense-looking guy.

"Well, there clearly is," Glen said. "But we can get into that tomorrow with the experts. Tonight, we have a campfire with the older girls' cabin." He rubbed his chubby hands together. "Maybe some sparks will fly."

Kyle thought back to the informal prom they'd had last year when he hooked up with a basketball player from Oregon behind the bleachers. He eyed Neal. Hopefully sparks would fly, all right.

● ● ●

Jem already hated Camp Genesis. Sure, she hadn't gone in with an open mind, but the first day already sucked hardcore. She was only at the hellhole because her dad wanted to avoid a lawsuit. Slugging that bitch Jennifer Goldberg in the face had been worth almost getting sued by her rich lawyer father. It was the first time she'd ever hit anybody, but Jennifer had been asking for it. Jem remembered with bitter clarity the day the cheerleader and her giggling coven had cornered her in the girls' room and called her a "dyke." They wouldn't let her leave.

It wasn't like Jem *wanted* to hit anybody, but Jennifer had blocked her way out, her lipstick-smeared lips crimped in a sadistic grin.

"Dyke," she'd accused, spitting the word like venom. Then the others took up the word, chanting it over and over. It echoed loudly in the bathroom. Jem saw red and slugged Jennifer. Then there was actual red, all over the cheerleader's white uniform. Her nose had a weird kink in it.

Like daddy can't afford to fix it for you.

23

Jem told herself to ride the camp out, agree with whatever nonsense the adults spouted off, and then get a girlfriend when she got back home.

Easier said than done, especially the girlfriend part.

After the older girls had settled into their cabin, a pretty blonde counselor named Michaela took them out to a clearing on the edge of the woods that creeped Jem out. She felt more comfortable in libraries or mosh-pits. Maybe that was why the girls at school hated her so much. They couldn't understand a girl who dressed the way Jem did—and she always got good grades. She was a freak.

Once they arrived at the fire pit, Counselor Michaela sat the girls down and said, "We're going to have a lot of fun. We'll have a nice, toasty fire, and we can roast marshmallows."

"Shouldn't we start the fire now?" one of the girls asked.

"We'll let the boys do that when they get here," Michaela said.

"I can start a fire," the butchest girl said. "No problem."

"I'm sure most of us can, but it shouldn't be too long," Michaela said. "We'll wait."

Once the eight boys had arrived with their counselor, Glen, they gathered wood and were given a quick lesson on starting the fire while Michaela pointed out how well the boys were doing. Glen soaked it up and slapped the guys' backs with each manly encouragement.

Jem tried to get comfortable on the log she'd staked out while a skinny blond boy cracked a joke about being an expert at gathering wood. She winked at Billy when he glanced at her. He looked miserable. At least there was one person who hated this place as much as she did.

When the fire was started, Glen ordered the guys to sit in between the girls, carefully arranging them boy-girl-boy-girl. They had to go around the circle, awkwardly introducing themselves. After marshmallows were skewered and thrust into the fire, Michaela got them all to say the Lord's Prayer again.

"I want you to really think about the words," she said.

They'd barely been there two hours and they'd already prayed more times than Jem had her whole life. Was that how Katherine planned on straightening everybody out? Brainwashing them with prayers? She was fairly certain the line was "love thy neighbor" and not "love they neighbor only if they neighbor is a heterosexual" but she wasn't about to get into it with the counselors this early.

Once the droning was over, Michaela shot a grin around the campfire and declared it was time to start the scary storytelling.

"I'm glad I got assigned the older campers. Otherwise, I wouldn't feel right telling you about what happened to my friend Jamie's cousin."

"What happened to Jamie's cousin?" one of the girls asked.

Sheep.

"She's trying to tell you," Jem pointed out.

"Oh. Sorry. Who's Jamie?"

"A friend from high school," Michaela said. "Anyway, her cousin, Samantha, is a few years older than me. After college, she moved into a new house in Philadelphia with one her of friends, Joan."

The butch girl snickered and Jem knew exactly what she was thinking. Sure, Samantha and Joan were *only* roommates.

"It was a great two-story place she was really happy in. One day, she was shopping downtown and she started flirting with the cashier at a bookstore. She mentioned where she was living and he went pale."

Next to Jem, Billy leaned forward, apparently intent on the story. She thought telling tales around the fire was kind of lame, but she was interested in what happened to this Samantha girl and her "roommate."

25

"The handsome cashier told Samantha he knew exactly which house she was living in, because that's where a double-homicide happened just one year before. In fact, it had been almost one year to the day. Samantha didn't want to let him know how spooked she was by the story, but she asked if they ever caught the killer. She found out the police were still investigating and no arrest had ever been made."

"This isn't going to end well," breathed Tommy, the nervous, mousy kid. He drummed his fingers along his thigh.

"Shut up and let her tell it," a short guy said as he plucked a toasty marshmallow off his stick.

"Easy, guys," Glen said placidly. "Go on, Michaela."

"Samantha told Joan about what she'd heard, but her friend wasn't very concerned. Still, Samantha couldn't stop thinking about the poor couple who had been butchered right in the home she lived in. Joan suggested if she was that worried that she get a guard dog. Samantha went down to the pound and adopted a sheepdog named Rex. He was a great cuddly dog who slept each night at the foot of Samantha's bed. Whenever she had trouble sleeping, or woke in the middle of the night, Samantha would reach down and feel comforted by Rex lapping at her fingers."

Kyle interrupted, saying, "Speaking of dogs, I heard my neighbor's friend got caught spreading peanut butter—"

"That's enough, Kyle," Glen said.

"Sorry."

Michaela continued her story while Jem and most of the others looked on edge, having forgotten their burning marshmallows.

"Late one night, Samantha woke with a start, her heart beating wildly. Had there been a crash? She reached down and felt the dog licking her fingertips and decided it had just been a bad dream. She fell back asleep. The next morning, Samantha woke up and walked past Joan's room on the way to the bathroom. Joan's door was wide open. Samantha screamed and nearly passed out."

"What did she see?" Billy asked.

"Joan was butchered in her bed, along with Rex. Something was written in blood on the wall: *humans lick too*."

A wave of horror swept through the teens sitting around the fire. The hair on the back of Jem's neck stood on end and she caught Billy looking over his shoulder at the dark woods behind them.

"Is that true?" Tommy asked.

"Of course it is," Michaela said.

"No way…"

"I know a story," the butch girl said.

Jem listened as the campers tried to one up each other and freak everyone out. She told herself it was stupid to get goose bumps over their stories, but she couldn't help it. With the darkness crowding in around their campfire, those horrible stories seemed somehow more plausible.

After a while, the goofy boy, Brady, ended the scary stories. "Hey, I want to know about what happened to the Camp Genesis buildings," he told Michaela. "I heard it used to be in a swanky farmhouse with indoor plumbing. What's up with that?"

"That's true," Michaela said. "When I was a camper, we helped out on the farm."

Jem's face lit up. She hadn't pegged Michaela as a former camper.

Don't get a crush on your ex-gay counselor. She's older than you, and apparently straight or something.

"I heard something horrible happened," Brady said. "What was it?"

Michaela paused a moment. "There was a fire," she said at last. "It took a little while, but then Katherine found this campground and rented it out. Anyway, that's enough for tonight.

We have a big day planned for all of you, right, Glen?"

"You betcha." Glen stood up and cracked his back, the campfire reflecting across his glasses. "Come on, boys, time for bed."

Jem watched the guys scramble away before contemplating Michaela through the dying flames. She couldn't help wondering what her counselor was hiding from them.

Chapter 4

Billy was finding it difficult to keep up with everybody's names. The one that stuck in his head was "Neal." It lit up his insides like it was flashing in hot neon.

Don't get another crush.

He was always attracted to guys who had no interest in him. All the way through high school, he'd had a thing for jocks. The only reason he'd managed to keep a lid on his sexuality for so long was because he was into football. Every game, every practice, every team meet, he was there, cheering and waving a giant foam finger. He'd even enlisted as waterboy last year.

He wasn't there for the football, though. Late at night, he fantasized about what went on in the locker room, but he was too afraid to ever go in.

Not that it mattered. The jocks all ignored him and the cheerleaders thought he was weird.

As they sat around the campfire, Billy watched Neal, wondering if he was like all the other jocks. He was here, wasn't he? That meant he'd had some kind of issue with his sexuality, even if he denied it.

When everybody had finished telling scary stories, the campers were encouraged to mingle and make friends. The mousy kid, Tommy, stuck to Billy's side like a magnet. A twang of annoyance shuddered through him when he noticed Neal talking to Kyle, the irritating, self-proclaimed king of Camp Genesis.

Kyle said something and Neal laughed. Billy's gut shriveled.

"You think that really happened with Michaela's friend's cousin?" Tommy asked.

Jem slapped him on the back. "Sure, and my uncle's an axe murderer and my gramps keeps Grandma locked up in the attic."

She winked at Billy.

"Don't worry so much," Billy told the younger camper. "We're going to make it through this together."

Tommy nodded, but Billy noticed him shiver as he peered at the woods. Billy thought he saw movement between the trees, but it was too dark to tell if it was an animal. He thought about the creepy guy who'd been staring at him during registration and a chill ran up his spine.

"This place couldn't be any different from New York," he muttered.

"Yeah, Bill, I should probably teach you some new words. Like 'tree' and 'lake' and 'fresh air.'"

"Funny, Jem."

Neal's laughter drew Billy's attention and he watched Kyle perform some terrible disco dance moves. It was going to be a long summer.

● ● ●

Tommy tried to stay as close to the other guys as possible on the short trek back to the cabins. The scary stories had bothered him almost as much as everything else at Camp Genesis. He wished he'd never told his pastor that he was starting to have funny feelings about some of the boys in Sunday school. He should have just kept it to himself. Camp Genesis terrified him. He wasn't the outdoorsy type, he hated meeting new people, and most of the guys were really hot. How was he supposed to get over being queer with so many guys around? They should have just sent him to an island for shock therapy.

When they reached their cabin, Counselor Glen said, "Take a seat on your beds. I have one last story for you guys before lights out."

"More stories?" Tommy's chest tightened.

"Yeah. Gather 'round." The guys clustered together on the bottom bunks and Tommy pressed up close to Billy.

Glen peered at them one at a time, his face grave. "One of my good buddies from high school was gay, but he never told anyone."

"Because society blows," Matthew said.

"No one blows enough," Kyle quipped.

"Because you don't have a steady guy," Brady said. "My neighbor, Stanley—"

"Let Glen talk," Neal said, glaring daggers at the others. Tommy was glad when they all quickly shut up. As much as he didn't want to hear the story, he also didn't want any extra tension in the cabin.

"Anyway, my buddy got engaged to a nice girl after graduation. We threw him a huge bachelor party, and he got wasted. He snuck out and had his own party. He was so drunk and horny that he paid a young hustler for sex."

"You can do that?" Cobb, the chubby guy, asked. Tommy had never heard the word "hustler" before, but he assumed it was another word for "hooker." He felt even more uneasy and tried to become as small as possible on the bunk.

"How much?" Brady asked.

"That's not the point." Glen sighed. "The point is, my buddy woke up in a cheap motel room the next morning with a pounding headache. The hustler was gone, and so was his wallet. My buddy looked around the room and found a message written in lipstick for him."

"What did it say?" Tommy breathed.

"Welcome to the world of AIDS."

A shiver ran through Tommy's body and, next to him, Billy shook his head.

"That's so messed up," Steven lisped.

"That really happened?" Cobb asked.

"Yep," Glen said. "So keep in mind, anytime you want a quickie from a strange guy, you could be hooking up with AIDS Harry. Okay, lights out in ten minutes, guys, so get ready for bed." He looked at Kyle and added, "Your *own* beds."

Tommy watched as Brady closed his eyes and held his hands up in the air like a blind man, asking, "Which bed is mine?"

"Real funny, but I'm serious," Glen said. He shot them all an *I'm watching you* look before disappearing into his private room next to the restroom.

Tommy looked around at the other seven boys in the room, hoping someone would say something.

"Should we, uh, take turns in the bathroom?" Billy asked, meekly holding his toothbrush in one hand.

"Go for it," Neal said with a smile.

Tommy wanted to join in the conversation, but he couldn't bring himself to say anything useful. Billy disappeared into the bathroom and Steven and Matthew formed a line.

"Um, what's everyone wearing to bed?" Cobb asked slowly. Tommy assumed the chubby boy was worried about the others picking on him.

"Well, I'm pretty modest with other guys around," Kyle said as he stripped off his shirt and then shucked out of his jeans. He had a lean, smooth body, and his light blue briefs left very little to the imagination. Tommy had never seen underwear that wasn't white, but he was even more impressed with Kyle's body. "Normally I sleep nude," Kyle added with a shrug.

"Uh..." Brady clearly wanted to say something, but he looked frozen in place.

"I have sweatpants," Cobb stated. "Gray, baggy sweatpants."

"Cool." Kyle flashed him a giant grin. He was ridiculously handsome.

Tommy realized he was starting to get an erection and felt queasy. He sat on his bed and held a pillow over his lap. His palms started to sweat and he couldn't believe his parents had forced him here.

• • •

After lights out, Tommy stared up at the ceiling, his eyes slowly growing accustomed to the dark. He couldn't stop thinking that there were seven other guys lying in bed in the same room.

Seven gay guys. Or five gay guys, a confused guy, and another in denial. Are they repressed? Am I? Do they like me? Is that wrong? Am I going to Hell?

He listened for any sign of life from the others. Cobb snored lightly on the bunk below and there was a symphony of steady breathing throughout the room. Tommy looked over to his only friend, Billy, as he lay on his side in the bunk over Neal.

I can't do this. I can't do this.

Tommy tossed the sheets off his body. Since he'd gone to bed in his jeans and a T-shirt, too embarrassed to bare any of his puny body, he was ready to sneak out. As quietly as possible, he swung his legs over to the side ladder and prayed he wouldn't wake anyone up. He'd get in so much trouble if Glen found him trying to escape Camp Genesis.

He'd been too panicked earlier to properly unpack, and so most of his clothes were still in a dirty red duffel bag pushed up against the edge of the bunk bed. He spotted it as he slowly descended to the floor.

Creak!

Tommy froze. He held his breath as he counted to twenty on the ladder, afraid to step down to the floor until he was certain everyone else was asleep. Finally, he hopped off the bed, adrenaline flooding through him. He grabbed his socks and shoes, then slung the duffel bag over his shoulders and tiptoed out of the cabin.

Once outside, Tommy stood for a moment on the porch and tried to get his bearings. He'd been too afraid earlier to pay much attention to the camp's layout. He shook his head and decided to just start running. As long as he got far enough in any direction, then he'd be free.

The blood pounded in his ears as he hurried away from the cabins and into the dark woods beyond. At first, he thought he was on a pathway, but he soon ventured off it. Branches slapped at his face and slowed him down to a crawl.

Tommy's duffel bag snagged on a heavy branch and he had to break it off to continue. He finally found the footpath again, but he wasn't sure which direction would lead him away from camp.

Great, I'm going to end up running around in circles until the sun comes up.

A twig snapped several feet away. Tommy froze. Could it be a wild animal? A *rabid* wild animal? He tried to remember what he should do. Sometimes it was best to play dead, but other times it was best to run as fast as you could. His legs were already starting to ache, but he prepared himself to book it if he had to.

"Hello?" he asked the dark forest. "Is anyone there?"

Another branch snapped, this time nearer than before.

"I'm sorry I ran away," Tommy said. "I just don't think this place is right for me."

Please let it be a person, please let it be a person.

The branches off the path parted and a dark figure appeared. He, or she, wore a baggy sweater and a baseball cap. Tommy couldn't tell who it was in the darkness.

"Are you taking me back now?" Tommy asked, his shoulders slumping.

The figure's head shook slowly. Tommy remembered Glen's creepy story about AIDS Harry and his skin crawled again.

"Oh. Well what's going on then?"

The figure held up a heavy-looking log and slammed it against Tommy's head. The blow nearly sent him to the ground. His vision blurred and his ears rang with pain.

Tommy called out and dropped his duffel bag. He tried clearing his head as he ran away from his attacker. He couldn't believe someone was trying to hurt him. The others had talked about a fire at Camp Genesis when it was at a farmhouse, and he had the feeling there was more to the story the counselors weren't sharing…

He stumbled over a root and crashed to the ground. Whimpering, Tommy spun around on his ass and backed away from the approaching figure.

"Please," Tommy cried out. "Don't hurt me. I'm sorry. I'm so sorry."

The figure reached him and batted the log against his head. The last thing Tommy ever heard was the deafening crack of his skull shattering.

Chapter 5

July 17, 1986

Kyle had never been a morning person. He was much more of an enjoy-the-night kind of guy, so when the scream of a whistle blasted him awake, he sat bolt upright and his head nearly slammed into the bunk above him.

"What gives?" he groaned sleepily, peering out from his bunk.

Glen lowered the whistle from his lips and Kyle saw that most of the campers were already in various states of dress—Billy had one leg in his shorts, and Neal was on the floor doing push-ups.

Fat Cobb, Kyle and the nerdy black kid, Steven, were the only campers still in bed. Groggily, Kyle watched Neal hop up from his push-ups, already dressed in khaki shorts and a gray T-shirt.

Dammit, I missed his morning shower.

Kyle had tried picturing Neal naked, or at least shirtless, but he couldn't tell if the stud would have any dark hair across his muscled chest or be smooth. He'd hoped to watch him enter or leave the bathroom in a fluffy white towel, but that annoying Billy kid was probably the only one who'd had the luxury of sneaking a peek. He noticed the nerd was practically drooling as he chatted awkwardly with Neal.

Glen blew his whistle again and Kyle finally tumbled out of bed.

"You wore that to sleep?" Glen asked, gesturing toward his skimpy blue briefs.

"What? They're designer," Kyle said. "Uh, girls would really like to see me in them. Very impressive."

"I'll say," Matthew said. It was the first thing he'd said that wasn't broodingly intense.

Kyle smirked.

"That's a positive step," Glen said. "I want you up and showered and ready to go ASAP. We have our first morning activities in thirty."

Kyle tried listening to Glen, but he couldn't help but watch the moony-eyed Billy as he practically fell over himself chattering at Neal. To his credit, Neal seemed to humor him without paying too much attention.

"What activities are we doing today?" Brady asked. "I'm used to waking and baking, but I'm guessing that's off the menu."

"Yeah. It's breakfast, then fun, gender-sensitive activities," Glen said with a look of excitement. Kyle thought back to last year's activities and shuddered.

"I was wondering," Neal said, "would it be too much trouble if I went home at night? Maybe my mom could pick me up or I could get a bike and commute myself. I won't miss any of the mandatory activities, honest."

"Sorry, kid, but that's not gonna happen. Hey, anyone seen Tommy this morning?"

● ● ●

Glen escorted the seven boys to the mess hall where they grabbed plates of greasy breakfast and sat around wooden tables spread out across the large room. The rough-looking cooks made fag jokes as they plopped food on trays. On his way over to Neal, Kyle passed younger campers who looked lost and depressed.

Billy was already sitting on Neal's other side with Brady and the purple-haired girl, Jem.

"I can't believe Tommy flaked so soon," Brady said as he dug into his eggs and hash browns.

No big loss. Kyle rolled his eyes as he skewered scrambled eggs on his fork.

"He did look really pale yesterday," Billy said.

"He probably just ran into the woods to get some space," Jem said. "I'm sure he'll pop up later today feeling stupid for making everyone worry."

"I guess so," Billy said. "I mean, I guess I shouldn't worry about him so soon, right?"

"Exactly," Neal said. "It's only been a few hours. I wouldn't sweat it until nightfall."

Let the kid worry, Neal. It's so not attractive.

"I wonder if Katherine's switched up activities or if we're following the same schedule as last year," Kyle mused.

"Oh, yeah, you're the resident expert on Camp Genesis," Brady said, shoving him with his elbow. "What should we expect from our goose-stepping camp owner?"

"I don't want to ruin the surprise."

"Come on, what do they have planned?" Neal focused his bright blue eyes on Kyle.

"Uh…" Kyle felt like he was melting a little under Neal's gaze. "If I remember correctly, they split up the boys and girls."

"Why?" Cobb asked as he sat with them, his plate piled high with food.

"To teach girls how to be girly and boys to be boy-ly."

Neal snorted and shook his head.

"You already have being manly covered," Billy told Neal. The jock turned to the nerd and smiled.

Damn it, Billy.

After breakfast, Katherine held another prayer session, and

told everybody to really commit to the activities. As everybody scraped their leftovers into the trash, she ordered the ladies to stay in the mess hall for cooking lessons while Father Oliver escorted the boys outside to the field.

Kyle sat on the grass next to Neal, with Billy on the jock's other side, and tied a knot in the bottom of his shirt to cool down in the blazing summer sun. He leaned back, showing off his flat stomach and enjoying the looks from the other guys.

The kids from the younger boys' cabins lounged around on the ground while the counselors finished setting up an intimidating-looking obstacle course on the field.

"This is going to be fun," Father Oliver announced. He wore a plaid shirt and a cross around his neck. "We're going to have the first in what we call the Camp Genesis Games. There may be trophies involved."

"Cabin Four for the win!" Glen shouted, pumping a fist in the air.

Neal flexed and stretched his muscular body, looking primed to compete, and Kyle sighed. He was going to have to at least try if he wanted to impress him.

He didn't remember starting with athletics last year, but maybe he'd blocked it out. He raised his hand and asked, "Is it just cabin against cabin, or do we compete individually?"

"Both cabins will have an MVP," Father Oliver said. Kyle gave him a blank look, so he clarified, "Most valuable player."

"Cool." Kyle shot Billy an evil look to psych him out and was pleased when Billy started nervously fidgeting with his laces.

"First up, we've got a timed obstacle course," the priest said.

"This is going to show you how much fun athletic competition can be," Glen stated. "So much better than theater or sewing."

"Nothing gay about athletics," one of the other counselors said.

Kyle thought about rugged guys wearing tight shorts, slapping each other's asses and then showering together, but he chewed on his lip to keep from saying anything since Neal was so into all of that. Glen led the boys in stretches and then they cheered each other on while they ran the obstacle course.

Kyle waited until after Billy had struggled through to run the course. He had to navigate through tires, jump over hurdles, and climb a wall while Glen timed him on a stop watch. He just hoped he could beat Billy's time.

"Good job," Neal said, slapping him on the back when he'd finished.

Huffing for breath, Kyle gave him a weak thumbs up. Neal stretched for a second and then tore through the obstacle course in no time. Cobb still lay on the ground, red faced and panting. It was probably the first exercise he'd done since fat camp.

"Is their plan to make us too exhausted to fool around?" Brady asked Kyle.

"Something like that."

Once everyone had run the obstacle course, Father Oliver announced Neal had the best time, to no one's surprise. Matthew and a few of the other guys looked disappointed, but Billy congratulated him before Kyle could.

Damn it, Billy.

Next, the campers squared off in tug-of-war, pitting the cabins against each other. Cobb anchored their team, followed by Neal, and then Kyle sandwiched in after him and before Brady. Kyle tried focusing on the strong cord of rope in his hands, but it was difficult with Neal's body so close to his.

"We can do this," Neal said quietly into Kyle's ear.

"Okay," Kyle said, trying not to swoon. He braced himself and waited for the blow of the whistle to start the match.

After a few seconds, they started pulling the rope taut. Kyle kept his eyes locked on his own hands as he pulled, trying not to worry about the other team. Someone shouted and Kyle felt the pressure on the rope increase. He realized Cobb had tripped and let go.

Damn it, Cobb.

"Come on, guys," Neal shouted. He leaned forward as Kyle pulled back and their bodies rubbed up against each other.

Kyle was so flustered he almost let go of the rope, but he managed to hold on and pull his share. One of the guys on the other team fell back and he heard Matthew grunting like an animal in heat.

"We have a shot at this, boys," Steven yelled, his lisp coming through as strong as ever.

"Wait a second, I don't care about tug-of-war," Brady said.

Neal started to tell him not to let go, but Brady shrugged and stepped away from the group.

"Damn it, Brady!" Neal hollered.

Kyle's forearms burned, but he vowed he wouldn't earn Neal's wrath and get a *damn it, Kyle* from the hot boy pressing his well-toned body against him.

"Count of three, and then give it everything you have," Billy yelled.

"Who made you team captain?" Kyle grunted.

"Three."

"Right, Neal?" Kyle asked.

"Two."

"Slow and steady," Kyle added.

"One."

Kyle sighed and tugged with all his might. The boys from the other cabin were yanked forward and collapsed in a heap on the ground.

Kyle threw down the rope, his fingers stinging. He turned around to hug Neal in celebration, but Billy stepped right past him and Neal grabbed him in a tight bear hug.

Damn it, Billy.

"Good job, guys," Brady said, and then shot pretend air guns at them.

"You did nothing," Matthew sneered.

"What? I removed a weak link. Obviously. Yeah, number one homo team!"

"I'm not gay," Neal reminded them.

"So, we're done now, right?" Cobb asked.

"There's still some races and other games we have to compete in," Kyle said.

"Oh, Christ."

"Cobb…"

"Sorry, Father Oliver."

Chapter 6

The setting sun painted the sky a vibrant pink above Camp Genesis, which Billy thought was sort of fitting. With Glen nowhere to be found, the guys inside were joking around, screaming, and roughhousing. Neal bragged about being the cabin's MVP, and Kyle lounged in his underwear on his bed. Billy had taken one look at the carnage and decided to get some fresh air. Leaning against the side of Cabin Four, he stared up, watching flocks of birds roll in the air above the forest, performing their dusk-time dance.

Dancing. Prom.

Kyle had mentioned something about an end-of-summer prom at last year's camp session—Kyle had hooked up with a tall guy with a tattoo—and assumed there would be another prom this year. The thought filled Billy with dread. His last high school prom, he'd gone with his friend Kristy, but only because her boyfriend had just dumped her for his second-cousin. Billy thought she had dodged a bullet there, but Kristy was devastated. Billy had been forced to sit and watch her mope, watery-eyed, as her ex whisked across the dance-floor with somebody else. He'd tried to cheer her up, but then he saw Mikey Munroe making out with the prom queen and he couldn't think of any reason to enjoy the dance. Maybe Jem would be his date to the camp prom?

Heh, camp prom. Aren't all proms campy?

Of course Neal would be his first choice, but that wasn't ever going to happen; not here. Maybe not anywhere. He wondered if he and Neal could meet up sometime after camp was over.

Who am I kidding? He's the king of this place. He'd never be interested in me.

Billy was so lost in his thoughts he didn't hear the crunching of heavy boots approaching.

"Jeez, you look like somebody died."

Billy nearly jumped out of his skin.

"Jem!"

"Skittery, too," Jem observed. "Don't ever change, Bill, you're adorable just the way you are. Sounds like *Lord of the Flies* in your cabin."

"I know. I'm waiting for Kyle to push a boulder on Cobb."

Her purple hair was even more unkempt than usual; it looked like she'd back-combed it like Madonna, though Billy suspected she just hadn't washed it since she arrived. She looked naked without her many bangles and bracelets, and Billy wondered if they'd been confiscated by the counselors.

Yeah, because bangles are what make you gay.

"How was today?" he asked.

"Like getting rammed through a Barbie-making machine ass-first. Only worse."

"What did they do to you?"

"While you guys were playing Conan the Barbarian, Katherine gave us beauty and house-cleaning tips. Then we got seamstress and baking lessons. Seriously, though, who died?"

"Nobody, but Tommy's still missing. And most of his clothes are gone."

"Aw, the baby? Think he jumped the fence?"

He shrugged. "Dunno, but nobody's doing anything about it."

"And?"

"And I think we should. He's just a kid; God knows where he is. What if he tried to escape through the woods and he fell and broke something? He could be stranded out there calling for help, only nobody's around to hear it."

"That's some imagination," Jem said. "You should write for *Dallas*."

"What about that guy?"

"What guy?"

"The one from the main hall when we arrived. The weird one."

"The bum?" she asked.

"Yeah. I saw him go into the woods. What if he's done something to Tommy?"

"Now you're sounding more like *Dynasty*."

"I'm serious!"

He came close to stamping his foot, but he knew Jem would never take him seriously if he did that.

"You really are worried," Jem said, the usual glimmer in her eyes dulling slightly. He must look pretty bad to make her face do that. "The guy from the main hall is Norton Toombs. I overheard the counselors talking about him earlier. He's harmless, according to them. He's just a drunk vet getting by as a caretaker."

A vet? Maybe he's killed people.

"Doesn't mean he didn't do something to Tommy."

"What do you propose, General?"

"It's not too dark. Let's head into the woods and look for him. If we don't find him by dinner, we'll come back. What's to lose?"

The woods were the only place Tommy could have gone. That's all there was around the campground—woods as far as the eye could see. That, and the lake. Billy didn't want to think about that possibility, though.

Besides, if Tommy had drowned, he'd have been found pretty quickly. He couldn't help but picture the scrawny boy's body bloated and floating on the lake. He prayed he wouldn't find any corpses at Camp Genesis.

Jem rolled her eyes. "Fine," she said. "But only 'cause it's you. Just let me go change into my orienteering outfit." She looked deadly serious, but then nearly doubled over laughing. "Kidding! Jeez, if looks could kill…"

Together, they skirted around the back of Cabin Four and plunged into the woods. The change in atmosphere was immediate. The trees cushioned the sounds of the camp, and they couldn't hear the screaming and arguing from inside the cabin, which had been almost deafening just moments before.

"Spooky," Jem breathed.

Yeah. Is this a bad idea? They didn't really have any other choice. If Tommy was hurt, he needed them, and Billy couldn't let some spooky trees get in the way of that. He looked around the forest for any sign of the younger camper. He suddenly felt very far away from home. The closest thing to this in his neighborhood was a park, which only had about a dozen trees. Billy felt totally out of place.

He thought of Jake, his five-year-old brother. If it was Jake lying hurt in the woods, he wouldn't hesitate.

Man up.

"So, you seen anybody you like?"

Billy was grateful that Jem had broken the eerie silence, but that wasn't exactly a question he wanted to answer.

"I knew it!" Jem laughed, pouncing on him. "Who is it? I bet I can guess."

"It's nobody." He shrugged her off and avoided her eye. "Let's just look for Tommy, okay?"

"You're smitten!" Jem shrieked. "At least you've got some eye candy. The best I've got is Michaela, and an ex-gay counselor's not exactly an easy lay."

Easier than Neal, I'm sure. He doesn't even want to admit he's gay.

Jem grabbed his arm, and Billy froze.

46

"Listen," she whispered.

He strained to hear.

"What—"

Jem clamped a hand over his mouth.

There it was. A crunching sound. Like boots crushing dead leaves. There was nobody around, though. Nobody he could see. With Jem pressed up against him, he searched the surrounding area. Nothing.

"You, kids!"

Billy screamed. He couldn't help it. The gruff voice had come from behind them, and they spun toward its owner.

"The bum," Jem hissed in his ear.

It was the man from the main hall. Norton Toombs. He looked scruffier than he did before. Possibly in his thirties, he wore a stained tank top and dog tags. He had a military-style buzz-cut and he squinted blearily through bloodshot eyes.

"What are you kids doing out here?" Toombs swayed slightly as he stomped through the undergrowth, grabbing at trees as he went.

Drunk.

"What's it to you?" Jem demanded back.

"Kids aren't allowed in the woods," the man barked. "Too dangerous."

"And here we were hoping to make friends with Bigfoot," Jem drawled.

Toombs staggered closer. He lugged his left foot behind him like a dead weight.

"Smart mouth, she's got," he slurred, squinting at Jem. "Won't be so smart when she's dead."

"Is that a threat?"

Billy had to hold Jem back; she looked like she was about to hit the guy.

Toombs cackled, then grew suddenly serious. "Get the hell

out of here," he roared, anger sparking in his bloodshot eyes. Billy got a whiff of him and had to turn his head. "Get out, or it's your funeral!"

"What have you done to Tommy?"

Billy realized he was the one who'd yelled this time. He couldn't keep it in. He had to know if Toombs had hurt the younger camper. He seemed unhinged enough. Probably lived out here in the woods and hunted kids who strayed away from the camp.

Toombs looked confused. "That a friend of yours?"

Billy nodded. "He's missing."

The color drained from Toombs' face and he seemed to emerge from the mania. "Christ," he muttered, only just loud enough for them to hear. "It's started already." He looked at them. "Go back to the camp. *Now*. And don't ever come back into the woods."

"Come on, Billy, he's just a crazy old drunk," Jem said, pulling him away from Toombs. "Catch ya later, Toombs." She flipped him the bird over her shoulder.

Billy didn't know what to think. He was even more scared of Toombs than before, but it seemed like the drunk had never heard of Tommy. Maybe he hadn't strung him up in his shack and skinned him alive, after all.

They hurried away through the woods and didn't stop running until they were back at the cabins.

Chapter 7

Billy stepped into the shower and savored the feeling of the water pounding his shoulders. He felt filthy after their forest encounter with Toombs. Campers were only supposed to have one shower a day, something about preserving water supplies, but this was an emergency. He just had time to sneak a quick wash in before dinner.

As the steam filled up the stall, his thoughts turned to Toombs. Jem had heard the caretaker was harmless, and his leg seemed pretty bad, so he wasn't exactly mobile. Could he really be responsible for Tommy's disappearance? Billy sort of hoped he was; at least then they'd know.

If Toombs wasn't responsible, who was?

Even in the hot shower, the thought made him shiver. If Tommy hadn't run away, what had happened to him?

Billy wondered if Tommy had done something to piss Katherine off. She was ruthless, but was she powerful enough to make an unruly camper disappear without a trace? And Tommy was hardly the unruly type...

He shoved his face under the water and washed away the forest dirt he imagined was plastered all over him.

A sound came behind him. Almost like the shower curtain being drawn back.

He spun around. His vision was blurry from the water but he made out a figure standing looking at him.

"Want company?"

It was Kyle.

Night Terrors

Billy rubbed at his face, his vision clearing.

"Kyle, get outta here," he said, covering his modesty with his hands.

"Honey, please, I've seen more cocks than a chicken farmer." Kyle's laugh was weirdly humorless.

"Seriously, get outta here."

Kyle leaned against the tiled wall and looked him up and down, from toes to sopping black hair.

"Look at you, all naked and vulnerable," he said coldly. "Skinny little city boy."

The water beat against Billy's back and he thought about pushing past Kyle to grab his towel from the hook just outside. There was something about the way Kyle looked at him, though, that made him stand and wait, his hands cupped around his genitals.

"Back home, I chew up guys like you in my sleep and spit you back out again," Kyle said. "You think I'm going to compete with you. You're so, so wrong."

"What are you talking about?"

"You know exactly what I'm talking about. Or, you know, *who*."

Billy didn't understand. He was competition? For who? He didn't even like…

Neal.

Did Kyle like Neal, too? He'd noticed Kyle checking the jock out, but he'd noticed Kyle checking out just about every guy in the cabin at one time or another. Either sizing up the competition or getting a good eyeful.

"I don't—" Billy started.

Kyle raised a finger and pointed it at him.

"You're nothing, okay?" he said. "You're not even on his radar. Besides, you couldn't handle him even if he was into you. Not that that would ever happen."

"I—"

"He's mine," Kyle said firmly. "He might not know it yet, but he is. Just stay away from him."

He held Billy's gaze a moment longer before turning to leave the shower stall.

"Oh, you want this?" he asked casually, plucking the towel off its hook. He passed it into the shower, but as Billy went to take it, Kyle dropped it onto the sopping stall floor.

"See you at dinner."

Billy stood shivering.

● ● ●

Norton Toombs carried his rucksack through the mud. Specks flew up into his left eye, but he didn't have anything to wipe it away, so he clenched that eye shut and kept going. Guns fired everywhere. Bombs in the air, explosions on the ground.

Screaming. Was it the enemy? His friends? Himself?

Blood. He didn't think so at first, but then he knew the blood was his.

Norton's eyes opened, although he felt the left one ticking. Was there still mud in there?

No, that was...years ago. That was across the world.

Norton swung his legs off the cot in his groundskeeper's shack, his vision adjusting to the dim light in the room. He scratched at his back and cracked his neck. How long had he been sleeping for? Two hours, maybe three. That's good enough. Sure beat when he first got back home and barely managed an hour a night.

It didn't help that his mom teared up most mornings when she saw him limp into the kitchen, scruff on his face and an untrusting look in his eyes. How could he trust anyone when they gave him that look?

Norton's eyes drifted to the half empty bottle of vodka on a side shelf. He wanted to lose himself in the cheap bottle, but he wasn't supposed to drink while he was staying at the camp. The deal was he would dry out and help the kids.

Help kids.

He snorted at the thought.

Rich people's problems. Oh, my son likes to suck dick. Boohoo. My little girl is a carpet muncher. So what? They all end up face down in the mud. Everyone ends up in the dirt.

"You're all gonna die." Norton was surprised at the sound of his own voice. His eyes darted back to the bottle of vodka. He was thirsty...

It was better to work. Katherine had ordered him to keep the forest at bay so there was always trimming to be had. And creaking steps. And leaking faucets.

Norton ran a calloused hand over his buzzed hair and ordered himself to relax. He could get some work done and then, maybe, reward himself with a drink.

But work will go faster after I've had one or two.

He closed his eyes and saw dead friends in the mud. When he opened his eyes back up, he was pouring vodka into a mostly-clean cup. He cracked open a warm Mountain Dew and filled the glass up to the top, nearly half the can.

The drink stung the back of his throat, but in a good way. He savored the familiar taste like greeting an old friend.

"One drink, then work."

He sat on the edge of his bed and grabbed a yellow pad of paper, checking the to-do list Katherine had given him. His notes were scribbled all over it. Notes and doodles of guns and explosions. There was a little reminder to write to the pastor at his mother's church and thank him for hooking him up with the job. He'd written the address somewhere.

He glanced at his work reminders. Trim the hedges. Fix the pipes. Check the fly strips. Mow the field. Clean out the old boathouse—that one he kept putting off since he didn't relish the idea of trudging all the way out there to combat the spider infestation. Stay sober.

Someone knocked on the door of his shack.

"Yeah?"

No one answered. Norton took a swig of his vodka and Mountain Dew and set the cup down. Had he imagined it? He'd hoped the auditory hallucinations would end while he was so secluded from the rest of the world.

Knock, knock, knock.

"Who's there?" Norton limped to the door and threw it open. He was met with a darkening sky and a gentle breeze. "God damned kids."

Grumbling to himself, Norton slammed the door and returned to his cup. He finished his drink and then poured in more vodka, followed by the rest of the Mountain Dew.

"Don't want to leave this out to go flat." He took a sip and then massaged his bad knee.

Knock, knock...

"Dammit, who's there?" Norton slammed his cup down, spilling some of it, and stormed to the door. He pulled it open, but there was no one outside. He licked his lips and took several steps away from the safety of his shack. "This prank isn't even clever, it's just irritating. I'm trying to get some rest before I get back to work."

Snarling, Norton circled his shack. He couldn't wait to find whoever was bothering him and drag his sorry ass to Katherine's office. Let the kids be afraid of him; better that than pissing him off even more every day.

"Show your ugly homo face and this will go a lot easier on you!"

Norton paused. Was that his own voice? Had someone really been knocking? Sometimes, he just wanted to knock the shit out of those snot-nosed kids. Sometimes, he wanted to take a branch and slam it against their skulls until they stopped twitching.

"You're all gonna die."

He sounded like his supervising officer. But his officer was dead. They were all dead.

"We're all going to die."

Norton came back around to the front of the shack and opened the door. He shuffled back inside and spotted his empty cup. Had he really drunk it already?

"One more drink, and then I'll get to those faucets in Cabin Three."

Norton crossed the dark shack to his bed but the vodka bottle was gone.

"Get it together, man."

Norton turned around to look for the vodka when the glass bottle smashed against the side of his head. Glass shattered everywhere and he felt a warm ooze creep down his face. He thrashed out at his attacker, but he could barely see anything.

The attacker didn't say a word, just backed up and then slashed out with the broken bottle. It sliced Norton's arm. He tried swinging, but he felt dizzy and he couldn't move fast enough on his bad leg.

Norton's attacker shoved him down and then pinned him to the dusty floor. Norton struggled against him, but he already felt woozy. He heard himself calling out, shouting obscenities that didn't make any sense.

And then the bottle was plunged into the side of his neck. Blood sprayed out from the wound and he knew it was too late. The glass shard in his eye felt like mud and he thought, *We're all gonna die.*

Chapter 8

Michaela sat alone in her counselor's room, going over paperwork for Katherine while she listened to her charges gossip and get to know each other in the main cabin. The girls were still comparing their accents and talking about their hometowns. Maybe after a few weeks, they'd start talking about the boys. Michaela thought they'd be better off bonding without an adult around.

Since when am I an adult?

She checked the alarm clock next to her bed and saw that it was almost dinner time. She remembered what it was like when she'd attended the Genesis program four years ago after her mother caught her making out with her study buddy, Gail. It was the last time she ever talked to Gail.

Michaela had been so afraid to go to Genesis, but her mother insisted, and her mother never took no for an answer. She'd fallen in love with the farm and learned to work the land. Katherine was warmer back then, and her husband so nice. The summer started out really awkwardly, with the girls shy and the boys even shier, but then she made friends and let the program work for her.

Then came the fire, waking them up in the middle of the night. Her garden burned and the Creeveys had to find a new location.

After setting down her clipboard, Michaela took a deep breath and opened the door. The eight girls on the other side immediately fell silent. They stared up at her, and she tried to think of their names as she surveyed them.

"Hey, all. Time for dinner. Hope you're hungry."

"Is it going to be better than yesterday's slop?" Jem asked.

"It's probably what's left over from yesterday," Michaela said with a sideways grin.

"Great."

Some of the other girls grumbled and Michaela felt like she was already losing them. They were young, they didn't want to be there, and they weren't yet receptive to the program. She tried to remember a few years back when she'd been at camp and what she thought of her counselor.

At the time, their counselors had been all over them in that wonderful old farmhouse. Aside from the privacy the campground offered, the current Genesis program was mostly the same, with gender-specific games and lessons from adults and clergy. A few of the girls hooked up and were kicked out of camp. Michaela had been jealous of them initially, but that was before she accepted her inner heterosexual.

She left the program after the fire, but the program never left her. The only time she ever doubted it was that next summer, when she heard about poor Miles and that other boy. Even years later, Michaela could still picture Miles and hear him joking around with the other campers.

Swallowing hard, Michaela did what she did best—pushed out the negative thoughts. The summer would be great. She'd change the lives of kids for the better. And she'd even get a nice tan doing it.

"All right, girl talk time."

"Uh oh." Jem rolled her eyes.

"I was right where you girls are. Just four years ago. Confused, uncertain. Struggling with my parents and my church. But mostly, struggling with myself. But all of that changed when I came to camp. And it can change for you all, too. It's going to get better. And you know what, I didn't find peace in the cafeteria eating crappy camp food."

The girls were quiet. Jem looked like she wanted to say something snarky, but she kept her mouth shut. Had they finally seen Michaela how she wanted them to? As a role model, someone to emulate?

"That's really sweet, but is the food going to get any better?" Brenda asked.

"Maybe I can make an ice cream trip to town," Michaela suggested.

"All right!"

"Okay, campers. Let's get a move on." Michaela rounded them up and led them out of the cabin and toward the mess hall. Most of the rest of the camp was already assembled and kids and adults sat clustered in their cabin groups. Michaela nodded to Glen and then made her way to the serving line with her girls close behind her.

"Hey, good looking," the scruffy cook, Donny, said.

"Hi, Donny." Michaela surveyed him, and deemed him handsome enough, with a symmetrical face and short auburn hair. She glanced down and pushed her blonde hair behind one ear, like she'd been taught to do.

"How about you and me give the fruits a demonstration on the joys of straight fucking?" Donny leered at her and the girls behind her tittered.

"That's inappropriate."

"The language or the mental picture?" he asked.

"Both." She grabbed her food and hurried away from the cook as he chuckled with the others.

Once they were seated and started eating their mashed potatoes and meatloaf, Michaela shared a smile with Jem over the food. It really was bad.

Michaela noticed Glen and Katherine stepping up onto the

small stage in the front of the mess hall. She wondered if she was supposed to join them, but then Glen started speaking.

"Hey, everybody, quiet down!" Everyone stopped talking, but there were still some elbows thrown and forks scraping plates. "Katherine would like to talk to you all about something really neat."

Wonder if Glen has trouble breathing with his nose so far up Katherine's ass.

The thought shocked her, and Michaela tried to shake it off.

Peace and acceptance. Peace and acceptance.

Glen stepped back, and Katherine took his place in the center of the stage.

"Good evening, everyone. I hope you're all adjusting well to camp life." A wave of groans rippled through the room, but Katherine ignored them. "I want to tell you about a great program. We've decided to have an overnight camping party in a few days. Ice cream, s'mores, all of that good stuff. No gender activities, only talking and fun." That got applause, and a few wolf whistles, from nearly everyone. "Unfortunately, we'll only be taking campers who follow the rules. That means if you're caught doing anything you really shouldn't, you'll have to stay back at the cabins and do chores."

"Chores?" one of the guys asked.

"That's right, Kyle," Katherine said. "You should remember well from last year."

Some of the boys joked around, and Michaela shook her head. She wasn't sold on having a boy back who failed the camp last year. What if he was a bad influence on the others? He seemed nice enough from the little she knew, but she was sure he acted differently when adults weren't around. All teens did. She sure had with Gail.

Don't pre-judge him. He deserves help, just the same as everyone else. Maybe it's just supposed to take him longer to

58

accept it.

Katherine finished her announcements, and the kids started talking and playing around again. Michaela hoped none of her girls would do anything to warrant missing out on the overnight camping trip. She knew she'd be easier on them than Lisa was on the younger girls, but she really wanted them all to have a good time together.

Something banged across the mess hall, snapping Michaela out of her reverie. She looked over and found two of the older boys, Neal and Matthew, standing up from their table. Neal towered over Matthew, but both of his fists were clenched. Some of the guys hooted and egged them on.

Michaela looked around for Glen to take care of the situation, but he was nowhere to be seen.

"You shut your mouth!" Neal bellowed at Matthew.

"Make me, fruitcake."

Neal slammed his fist into Matthew's stomach. The other boys backed up. Michaela felt her fight or flight response gearing up.

"You stop that right now!" Katherine shouted, although she didn't move any closer to the fight.

Michaela hopped off the bench and hurried across the mess hall as Matthew dove at Neal. They rolled on the floor, kicking and punching each other. Michaela reached them as they continued pummeling each other, bent down, and pulled Matthew away.

"That's enough! What happened here?" She stared each boy down, practically daring them to cross her.

Neal sat up on the floor, giving Matthew a pissed-off glare.

"Well?" Michaela demanded.

"He called me some nasty names," Neal said.

"Which is not okay," Michaela said, turning to Matthew.

"It's not my fault he's in denial," Matthew said. "He can't

take a joke."

"I'm not in denial," Neal seethed. "There was *one* incident four years ago, and my parents won't let it go!"

Katherine and Glen finally reached them. No one else in the mess hall made a sound.

"Where were you?" Michaela asked.

"Bathroom," Glen said, the light flaring off his glasses. "Well, looks like we have our first two banned from the camping trip."

"What?" both boys asked, incredulous looks on their faces.

"Sorry, guys," Michaela said, thankful it hadn't been her call.

Chapter 9

Kyle leaned his head on his fist, watching Neal and Matthew slug it out on the floor. Most of the other guys frowned, shied away, or cheered them on, but Kyle wasn't interested. Neal would cream pipsqueak Matthew no problem if they were alone, but the counselors would break it up any second.

After Michaela pulled them apart, Glen showed up and banned them from the camping trip.

Kyle wasn't hungry anymore. He'd hoped the trip would be the perfect opportunity to get to know Neal better. They were supposed to do things biblically, weren't they? But now Neal would be stuck in the cabins doing chores while the rest of the camp roasted marshmallows and played pranks on each other.

Better him than me. Still, what a waste. Stupid Matthew can't keep his trap shut. It's obvious Neal's as queer as the rest of us, but you don't have to call him out on it. Let him act straight before and after the seduction.

Without Neal on the camping trip, Kyle would have to turn his attention to one of the other guys. He went through the mental checklist and despaired.

Matthew? Also banned, and too angry. Billy? No way. Cobb? Even worse. Steven? Too geeky. Tommy? Cute enough if he ever shows up again. Brady? Maybe if I'm drunk enough and he forgets about that neighbor guy he keeps going on about.

As Neal and Matthew threw themselves into their seats, Kyle overheard Katherine chastise Glen.

"Your boys couldn't go five minutes without breaking rules.

Makes me wonder about your whole cabin."

"What?" Glen looked horrified and adjusted his Coke-bottle glasses. "They'll be fine."

"We can talk about it later tonight," Katherine said. She gave the boys a once over and then strutted off. Kyle wished somebody would stick their leg out and trip her, but nobody did.

Pussies.

Glen sat down. "Good job, guys. Now I'm in trouble."

"I was just sitting here," Steven said. Billy and Cobb nodded.

Kyle rolled his eyes and told Neal, "You had Shorty, no problem."

"Thanks," Neal grunted.

"I would have put money on you," Brady said. "But I'm saving it for something special."

Glen scowled at them throughout the rest of dinner, so the guys mostly kept to themselves. Billy started talking about Captain Kirk and Spock to the other guys, and Brady made bad impersonations of TV stars, but Kyle kept out of it.

After dinner, Glen escorted the guys back to their cabin.

"All right, I have a counselors' meeting," Glen said. "I can trust you guys not to go all Kung Fu while I'm gone?"

"Or Kung Fuck," Brady whispered into Kyle's ear. He had to bite his bottom lip to keep from laughing.

"We'll be fine, sir," Neal said. "I'm awful sorry about before."

"Oh? Well, good." Glen nodded, as if he'd somehow counseled Neal. He checked his wristwatch and clicked his tongue against the roof of his mouth. "Meeting might go long. If I'm not back by lights out, you can stay up an extra ten minutes, but that's it. Deal?"

"Deal," Steven and Billy chorused.

Glen gave them a quick smile and then left the cabin.

"They leave us alone a lot," Cobb observed.

"Maybe it's a test," Steven said. "To see how we behave on our own. Do you think this place is bugged? We should be extra careful when Glen's not around."

"So you're telling me the orgy is cancelled?" Kyle mocked him.

"You keep talking like that," Billy said, "and you'll have to scrub the cabins while the rest of us are roasting marshmallows."

"Not all of us," Matthew grumbled. Kyle wondered if he ever turned down the intensity dial.

"Say, that's right," Cobb said. "I heard Katherine threaten that none of us can go."

"Katherine's all talk," Kyle said wearily. He wasn't afraid of the camp owner like everybody else. He'd seen it all before—this wasn't his first go round at Camp Genesis, after all. Just once he'd love to see Katherine Creevey really rattled. Maybe he'd try coming on to her; just to prove the camp really worked. That'd show her. But what if she took the bait? He shuddered at the thought.

"And how do you know?" Billy asked.

"'Cause otherwise I'd be doing the nasty with chicks now instead of listening to you whine."

Billy blushed. "I hate it here just as much as everybody else," he said, his cheeks growing redder by the second. "You don't have to be such a douche bag." Flustered, he brushed his dark hair behind his ears and then laid down on his bed, his back to Kyle.

Brady folded his arms and gave Kyle a disappointed look.

Kyle wasn't sure why, but he felt bad for being so cavalier with them. He didn't want to get all emotional, but he didn't want to watch them complain any more.

"Look," Kyle said. "I'll go see what Katherine's telling Glen. Then we'll know where we stand."

"And if you get caught, you're screwed," Cobb commented.

"I never got caught last year. I'll be fine, and even if I do get caught, you guys can pretend you had no idea. I'll be on my own, like on *Mission: Impossible*."

"This cabin will self-destruct," Brady joked.

"You sure you won't get caught?" Cobb asked.

"Uh, yeah. I'm a pro at sneaking around dark places, princess."

"That why they caught you and sent you here?" Matthew asked.

Kyle chose to ignore him. "'Bye, boys. Feel free to watch me leave." He spun on his heels and jiggled his ass on the way out.

A hush lay over the camp at such a late hour. Most of the lights were on in the other cabins, illuminating the netting at the windows, and Kyle could just about glimpse the movements inside. Everyone was supposed to be in their cabins, but he didn't want to risk any of the counselors or cooks spotting him. Or that creepy handyman Toombs.

Unless I can buy some booze off him. That might help loosen up Neal.

Kyle navigated past the campers' cabins and the mess hall, heading toward the main office, where Katherine stayed. There was a light on and he could hear someone talking.

Just then, Kyle spotted Glen and another counselor, Lisa, scampering down the path toward the lake.

Counselors' meeting, my ass.

Kyle considered turning back, but he had come this far, why not see what Katherine was up to? He continued on, hugging close to the side of the cabin, and peeked in through the window.

Katherine stood by her desk, wine glass in hand, while Father Oliver peered at the many antlers hanging from the walls.

"Why don't you have a seat?" Katherine asked. "Or some wine?"

"Yes to the seat, thanks. No to the wine."

Kyle ducked back away from the window as the priest moved forward. Luckily, the window was open to let in the evening air and he could still hear them talking.

"Any word from the police department on Tommy's whereabouts?" Father Oliver asked.

"They can't do anything until it's been forty-eight hours."

"That's ludicrous. The poor boy could be in trouble."

"He ran away. I'm sure the police will find him at any moment causing mischief in town," Katherine said.

"I spoke with him yesterday morning. Tommy didn't strike me as a mischief maker."

"No offense, Father, but you often only see them at their best."

And you only see the worst.

"I spent four hours this afternoon searching for him," Father Oliver said.

"You said you spotted his tracks leaving the camp?"

"I did. I also found them circling around and then ending abruptly."

"You're a priest, not a hunter," Katherine said. "Besides, if his tracks ended so abruptly, wouldn't you have found him right there?"

"I asked Norton to keep an eye out for him."

"Good."

"And now I can't find Norton, either," Father Oliver added.

Kyle frowned. Another missing person? The population of Camp Genesis was dwindling by the day. Had Tommy run off with the Toombs guy?

"No surprise there," Katherine was saying. "I'm sure he's in town at the seediest bar he can find."

"I'm not so sure about that. We've been talking. He shows real promise."

"You can't rehabilitate everyone, Father."

"Isn't that this camp's purpose?"

"Maybe he took pity on Tommy and brought him home," Katherine guessed. "It's not as if we can pick up a phone and reach people when they're out and about. This isn't *Star Trek*."

"I hope you're right. In the meantime, I think we should cancel the camping trip."

"Oh, no, no, no. We have a strict schedule. I have labored over the content of this summer program. Genesis works because of its structure. I don't want it falling apart like a house of cards."

"Katherine, I know the history of the Genesis program. I know your history."

What the hell does that mean? Katherine's history?

Kyle had never heard anything like that before. Did she have something to hide? He wouldn't put it past her. Somebody that tightly-wound was bound to have a few skeletons hiding in the closet.

"This has nothing to do with that," Katherine snapped.

"I'll be honest with you, Oliver, and I'll thank you not to bring that up again." She paused. Kyle heard a glass being refilled. "I want to keep this incentive to ensure the children behave. We take the camping trip away with all of its ice cream and promises of fun, and we'll be dealing with uncooperative beasts for the rest of the summer. They won't listen to us. They won't learn. And you know what happens if they don't learn. Their immortal souls are at stake."

"I know dogma," Father Oliver said. "But in this moment, I'm more concerned about their lives being in danger."

Chapter 10

Billy crushed Skeletor and let out a breath he'd been holding for almost the entire level. His *Masters of the Universe* video game was the only thing keeping him sane. He worried that Glen would confiscate it if he played too much, or suddenly decided it wasn't manly enough, so he kept it hidden at the bottom of his bag just in case. Camp Genesis seemed to revel in joy-killing to a near-prosecutable degree.

Weird, though, how completing a level wasn't satisfying enough—it only made him want to play more. There were probably studies into that sort of thing. He'd have to look them up when he got home.

He lay back on the top bunk, staring at the rough beams criss-crossing the ceiling. Kyle still hadn't returned from spying on Katherine and it was getting late. What if they caught him? Would they all get banned from the trip?

"Hey, Billy, what are you playing?"

Neal stood next to the bunk. *Does he really have to walk around topless so much?* Billy could barely keep his lustful thoughts in check as it was without Neal providing even more pec-flashing ammo.

"Nothing, it's stupid," he mumbled, slipping the hand-held console under the blanket beneath him.

"Stupid enough for you to play it every chance you get?" Neal wasn't mocking him, but grinning in a friendly way.

God, I want to kiss him.

Billy felt his throat start to burn and tried to rid himself of the lustful thoughts.

"Don't blame you," Neal said. He leaned an elbow against Billy's mattress, propping his head in his hand. "If I could escape from this place, even just through a game, I'd do it."

Billy didn't know what to do. He wanted to say something cool. Off the cuff. But awesome. Something that showed Neal he was intelligent and sexy and amazing. Perfect boyfriend material.

"I'd game all the time with the playing of games and He-Man is the best."

What just came out of my mouth?

Neal chuckled and picked a bit of fluff off the blanket. "He-Man, man. Now that's an uber-jock," he said, apparently unfazed by Billy's awkwardness. "Guy must spend hours pumping iron to get a body like that."

Billy wanted him to go away. No, not go away. Climb up onto the bunk and wrap him in those big, strong arms. Not talk. Just look at him. See him.

"You'd know."

Neal laughed again. "Nah, I *wish* I looked like him."

Before Billy could shove his foot even further into his mouth, Brady said, "Stanley doesn't look anything like He-Man, but he has a bigger sword."

Brady always seemed to find a way to insert his neighbor-boyfriend into conversations, as if Billy wasn't already jealous enough.

"Really?" Cobb asked wistfully.

Neal turned to the others and smirked. Billy worried he'd lost his bonding moment with his crush and searched for a way to get back his attention. Before he had the chance, Kyle burst into the cabin.

"I knew it," he yelled. "She's a total nutjob!"

Everybody, including Neal, turned to look at Kyle as he threw himself onto his bunk. Billy wrestled with a twinge of annoyance.

Kyle had drawn the attention all on to himself. Again. Now that Neal's blue eyes weren't shining on him, he came out of the daze. What had they been talking about?

"What are you yelling about?" Cobb asked.

"Katherine," Kyle hissed conspiratorially, grinning. "She was talking to the priest. She's a total cuckoo! He said she has a *history*. Probably drugs—or she's a raging muff diver. It would make total sense. She's in *total* denial! Oh, and somebody else is missing, too."

Billy sat up with a start, avoiding one of the wooden beams above his bunk by an inch.

"Who?" he asked.

Don't say Jem, don't say Jem.

Kyle directed his answer at Neal. "The bum, Toombs. He's vanished."

"You think he kidnapped Tommy?" Steven asked, putting down a comic book.

"Probably has a sex dungeon somewhere in the woods." Kyle nodded, as if it were an established fact. "This entire place is run by weirdos. Only a matter of time before one of them cracks."

Sex dungeon?

Kyle actually seemed to enjoy the drama.

"We better start getting Glen to lock the cabin door," he continued. "Don't want anybody coming in here at night and stealing our virginities."

"Too late," Billy muttered under his breath.

"At least I've had my lollipop licked," Kyle shot back. "All out of cherry flavor over here. Unlike some people."

Billy ignored him. Let him do the big talk thing; he wasn't impressing anybody. Unless Neal was impressed. Billy snuck a look at him and was relieved to see that Neal looked kind of bored. He scratched his armpit and then ducked down, disappearing into his own bunk.

"Guys, come on!" Kyle whooped. "This is huge! If we can prove Katherine's a kook, we can get this whole place shut down, and I won't have to spend a third summer here! Sayonara Camp Carnage!"

"Yeah, yeah," Cobb yawned, crawling into bed.

"It's late," Steven added. "I'm hitting the hay."

"You guys!" Kyle hollered. "Seriously? Neal? Brady?"

"If we shut this place down, it's off to rehab for me," Brady said. "I might actually learn something about myself there. No thanks."

"G'night, Kyle," came Neal's voice.

Billy got some satisfaction at Kyle being ignored. The guy could do with being taken down a peg or two. He watched Kyle huff and then strip off his clothes, climbing into his bed naked— but lingering by the bedside just long enough for Neal to get a look if he wanted to, Billy noticed.

Anything to shock. And he's well endowed, damn it. I may have some competition after all.

● ● ●

"Billy," a voice hissed. "Billy, wake up."

For one blissful moment, Billy didn't know where he was. The mattress beneath him felt like the one at home, and in the darkness he was sure he was surrounded by the walls of his New York bedroom.

Then he noticed the face craning over him and snapped to.

"Brady," he mumbled, still half asleep.

Brady shoved a hand against his mouth.

"Shhh!"

"What time is it?"

"Eleven, sleepy head," Brady said, as if it was normal to be wide awake in the middle of the night. "Get up."

"Go away." Billy tried to roll over, but Brady shook him mercilessly. "*What?*"

"I need you."

Rubbing at his sleepy eyes, Billy realized Brady wouldn't give up. He pushed the cover off and swung his legs over the side of the bunk. What did Brady want? If this was some kind of booty call, he wasn't interested. That said, Brady was cute in a lopsided sort of way... And Billy could do with the practice. He'd never even kissed a boy—seven minutes in heaven with Cindy Goddard when he was ten didn't count. But Brady had Stanley back home. Brady had talked about him so much, Billy felt like he knew the kid.

Blearily, he followed Brady to the door, comforted by Glen's snoring in the counselor's bedroom.

"All right, what?" Billy asked, noticing that Brady was already dressed in shorts, a T-shirt, a baseball cap and sneakers. "Where are you going?"

"Out, I found somebody who sells," Brady said, flashing him a cheeky grin. At Billy's bemused look he added, "Weed. I found a supplier in town before I checked in the other day."

"Great," Billy said sarcastically.

"And you have to come with me."

"Weed? You're waking me up for weed?" Billy exclaimed. "You know what, it doesn't matter what you woke me up for, because I'm not going out there."

People were missing, possibly kidnapped by a mad, drunken war vet, and Brady wanted to go out after dark? He really had been smoking too much pot.

"Neither am I, not alone. I don't want to end up sucked into a black hole like Tommy. If there's two of us, we'll be safe."

"That's crazy logic."

"The best kind."

Brady looked at him expectantly. Billy couldn't be convinced, though. The other boy's shoulders slumped.

"Shut up, you two," Matthew whisper-yelled from his bed.

"Sorry," Billy whispered back.

"Guess I'm going it alone, then," Brady said, pushing open the cabin door and disappearing into the night.

Billy stood there a second longer, wrestling with his conscience. He couldn't just let Brady go off, anything could happen to him, especially if he was going to spark up in the woods. Realizing what that meant, Billy rushed to the door and pushed his head out.

"Hey! Wait!" he hissed, finding Brady still waiting for him.

"Knew you'd come around," he said, sheepishly tugging at his cap.

"If we die, I'm gonna kill you."

Billy hurriedly pulled on yesterday's clothes, which were still in a heap on the floor by the bunk, and joined Brady outside.

"Think we should wake up Jem?"

"Are you mad? Three's only company when John Ritter's involved."

"Not allowed. Okay. She's the shit, though. She almost laid into Toombs earlier."

They were already out of earshot of the rest of the camp, which was lucky, because Brady let out a cry that was the very definition of *not subtle*.

"Toombs?" he hissed. "What the hell was she doing with Toombs?"

"We went looking for Tommy." Billy shrugged. "We found Toombs in the woods. He was acting pretty crazy."

"I'll bet. I heard the government gives soldiers LSD."

"Why?"

"I dunno."

They trudged underneath the camp's entrance sign. Billy

couldn't believe the lack of security. No wonder Tommy had no trouble running away. If that's what he did. There was no fence, no guards, nothing. It should have been a relief knowing that, but Billy only felt uneasy. If it was this easy to get out, it was this easy to get *in*, too.

Anybody could stroll into camp. Go into one of the cabins...

"So, what do you think of this place?" Brady asked.

"Sucks."

"Word." Brady glanced down the dirt track leading to the crooked mailbox that rested by the main road. "You think the mailman picks up every day?"

"I dunno."

"You miss home?"

Billy stiffened. *Home*. Just the thought of it made him feel hopelessly sick. He missed his brother, his room, his friends. Hell, he even missed his parents.

"Me, too." Brady smiled miserably. "I've never gone this long without seeing Stanley. I miss my fella." He smirked and threw an arm around Billy's slender shoulders. "We have each other, though. Think I'd have lost it by now without you guys. Hey, who's that?"

Somebody lingered by the woods at the side of the road. It was too dark to see him properly, but the way he stood, just watching them... Billy shivered.

"Maybe we should—" he began, but Brady was already calling out.

"Hey guy, you got it?"

The figure watched them a moment longer, and the way he was so motionless, so seemingly detached from everything around him, made Billy's skin crawl. A second later, the shadowy figure turned and disappeared between the trees.

"Hey! Where's my weed?" Brady yelled.

"Brady?"

They both jumped. Somebody had emerged right beside them. He was older—Billy could tell from the stubble and stained teeth—and totally grody. A townie, he figured. Must live nearby.

"You Brady?" the guy repeated.

Brady nodded hurriedly.

"Got the cash?"

Brady fumbled in his pockets and pulled out a couple of notes.

"Fifteen, right?" he asked.

"Twenty," the guy said. Brady didn't look happy about that, but he handed over three bills nonetheless and received a small bag in return.

"Nice doing business with—" he began, but the vendor had already started walking off. "Friendly round here, huh?" He grabbed Billy round the shoulders, dangling the bag in front of his eyes. "Want to have some fun?"

● ● ●

Jimmy grinned as he pocketed the twenty dollars.

Stupid kids. He ambled down the dirt track, away from that dumb-ass camp. He'd overcharged by five bucks, but he had a social life that needed upkeep. Besides, he'd driven all the way out there to complete the transaction. He deserved a little extra.

All he wanted was a cool beer in his hand and Martha's ample assets crushed against his ribcage.

The twenty-minute drive back to town would take forever. Luckily, he had something to take the edge off.

Jimmy reached behind his ear and retrieved a half-smoked joint. As he grappled with his lighter, the surrounding area briefly lit orange. Smoke curled from the joint and the darkness returned.

The van wasn't far off. He'd parked it where the main road

met the dirt track. He didn't want to disturb that Creevey woman. She came into town sometimes and he hated serving her at the store. Besides what the townies said about her, there was definitely something off. She gave him the creeps.

Creepy Creevey. That's what the guys in town call her.

He unlocked the van and got in. Twisted the key in the ignition.

Nothing.

He tried again. Still nothing.

"Christ's sake," he cursed, shoving his door open and going to the hood. He popped it up. "What the hell?"

The spark plugs were gone.

Damn kids. How had they managed to get there before him? Did they know he'd overcharged them for the stash? Well, he'd show them. He'd had plenty of years practice using his little brother as a punching bag. He knew exactly what hurt the most.

He slammed the hood down and a strangled cry of surprise left his throat.

Somebody sat in the truck. It was dark and Jimmy couldn't see the guy's face, but something about him sent a shiver down Jimmy's spine.

"Who's that?" he called warily.

The figure raised a hand and beckoned.

"Like that, is it?" Jimmy muttered, taking a final drag on his joint and then tossing it into the dirt. He went to the driver's door and wrenched it open.

"Look here, asshole!"

There was a flash of silver, and then hot liquid gushed down his chest.

Jimmy looked down and saw the blood soaking his shirt, though he could barely feel whatever was lodged in his jugular. He felt cold, suddenly. Desperately cold. As he tried to pull the object free, the figure in the car shoved him and he hit the ground.

Kids, he thought as the garden shears were raised over him. *Christ, I hate kids.*

Chapter 11

July 18, 1986

"This is sick!"

Jem rolled her eyes and shot Billy a look of disgust. She couldn't believe her parents had sent her here to endure this public humiliation. She'd be scarred for life. Which was sort of the point of Camp Genesis, right? To brainwash her? They wanted to make her forget what it was like to be an individual. She had to conform to herd mentality. Become a breeder. Their prize cow. Something to pop out a few grandkids, grow old and die miserable.

She even preferred the tedious cooking and sewing lessons to the current horror show.

"I think you look cute," Billy said, stifling a laugh, and she wanted to bury her knuckles in his face, but that's what had landed her in Camp Genesis in the first place.

The dress nipped at her shoulders and made a hideous *swoosh* sound whenever she moved. It was bright pink, constructed out of some sort of cheap theater material that shimmered but looked like something even a hooker would turn her nose up at. It itched all over, like she wanted to scratch out of her own body.

She spat on the ground and wriggled awkwardly, her blood boiling.

"Now, Jem, let's just go with it," Michaela said. "You might get something out of this if you don't fight it at every turn."

Jem huffed and forced herself not to look at the other girls, who were all slumped in equally-offensive costumes. The outdoor area by the lake had been turned into a makeshift theater.

The boys were dressed in ill-fitting suits and Jem was livid with jealousy. They were actually pretty stylish. Vintage. Or they would be if Jem wore them with her purple Converse and punked her hair up.

"Let's just get this over with," she muttered, grabbing Billy's hand and dragging him onto the stage.

"I'm supposed to lead, remember?" Billy hissed, but Jem didn't care. The dress was torture enough.

"Shut it, Romeo," she fumed.

Faux-meo is more like it.

"I want to feel the passion, guys," Michaela called, perched on a log and wearing a pair of glasses. She held a script in her newly-manicured hands. Jem couldn't help imagining her wearing *only* the glasses and directing her in a very different kind of play. "Remember, you love each other."

"You look very pretty, Jemima."

Katherine sat beside Michaela, observing the scene with the snooty look that made Jem hate being anywhere near her. And she'd used her full name, the evil bitch.

"Yeah, *Jemima*," called Kyle. "Who knew you could be such a lady."

"That's enough," Katherine snapped. "Let's start from the top."

Jem remembered to look down at her script. Something from *Romeo & Juliet*, naturally. What was this meant to teach them? That falling in love equalled death? It seemed the counselors had forgotten Shakespeare's star-crossed lovers didn't exactly live happily ever after.

"It's you first," Billy whispered. He looked cute in the suit, flattering his gangly limbs.

Billy scrubs up good. Still no way I'd give up the ladies for him.

He looked tired, though. Billy had told her over breakfast

about the midnight weed excursion with Brady. Maybe she'd try to score a joint off the stoner kid later. That'd take the edge off today's activity. When the breakfast tables had cleared, Billy told her something else about their trip. Somebody had been watching them from the woods. A creepy figure mostly hidden in the shadows.

"He just stood there, staring at us," Billy had said.

Jem shuddered. Something bad was happening at Camp Genesis—something more than the ritual humiliation. Both Tommy and Toombs were missing, and Billy had spotted a shady figure watching him.

Jem tried to forget about that. She looked at her script.

"Romeo, Romeo," she said, her voice coming out as bored as she felt. "Wherefore art thou Romeo?"

"Hot!" Kyle screamed.

Other campers wolf whistled and Jem wanted to use the dress as a camouflage. Yank it over her head and disappear inside its tasteless pink folds.

"Deny thy father and refuse thy name," she continued monotonously. "Or, if thou wilt not, be but sworn my love, and I'll no longer be a Capulet."

Billy stared dumbly at his script. Realizing it was his line, he jumped and called out flatly: "Shall I hear more, or shall I speak at this?"

Jem shielded her eyes from the sun. The dress's clingy fabric roasted her, like tinfoil. She glanced down at her skin to make sure it wasn't blistering. Not yet, but it surely wouldn't take long.

She peered at her script again. It wobbled in her vision like it was under water.

What was somebody doing lurking in the woods at midnight like that, anyway? Was it just a homeless bum? Or was it the person responsible for the disappearances at camp?

Camp Genesis was a nightmare, but she had felt safe here—

until now. If there was somebody attacking campers, who was next?

"'Tis but thy name that is my enemy," Jem murmured, attempting to focus on the swimming words. "Thou art thyself, though not a Montague."

Christ, Shakespeare's confusing.

Feeling hotter than ever, she glanced around for something else to focus on. She squinted over the heads of her audience. The lake. The water sparkled; a blanket of diamonds.

Wait, what's that? Somebody stood on the other side of the lake.

A figure had appeared on the far side. There were hardly any shadows, but the stranger was somehow bathed in darkness. He stood observing the gathering of campers. Despite the heat, Jem felt as if an ice cube was slithering down her spine.

Who was watching them? She couldn't make them out. Toombs? No, the figure was standing too confidently. She couldn't discern his face, but his ethereal eyes burned right into her.

It was the man Billy had seen last night. It had to be.

"You okay Jemima?" Kyle asked. "You look even worse than usual."

The lake stalker shimmered closer in the blinding light.

She couldn't breathe.

"Bill—" she began.

She couldn't handle the heat any longer.

She was vaguely aware of somebody saying her name. Of her hands clawing at the dress. Of her skin catching fire. Itching. Squeezing her tight until there was no air, even though they were outside.

And the sun was huge, filling the sky, filling her vision. Blinding her. Then it was all around her. Blazing. Burning. Cooking her alive. And there was nothing else.

● ● ●

Something damp rested on Jem's forehead.

Instinctively, she yanked it off and sat up. She was back in Cabin Two, laid out on her bed. The flannel in her hand was warm and moist.

"What the hell?" she murmured.

"Oh!" Michaela was sitting by her bed. She put down a book with a cave on the cover and took the flannel from her. They were completely alone. "I've been so worried. How are you feeling now?"

Jem touched her pounding head. Her mouth was unbelievably dry.

"What happened?" she asked, gratefully taking a glass of water from Michaela.

"The heat got to you. Either that, or you took the drama class more seriously than anybody else. I've never seen anything like it."

The play. Billy in the suit. That dress.

Jem looked down. She was still in the dress.

Dammit.

"Yeah, you can repair the damage in textiles class," Michaela said. Jem noticed that the neck of the hideous theater costume was ripped, as if somebody had torn desperately at it.

Or I did.

"I'm such a freak," she muttered. Suddenly Michaela's hand closed over hers and Jem met her eyes in surprise.

Michaela squeezed her hand. "It may feel that way, but we're here to help you."

Jem's stomach fluttered and her temperature rose again. Something seemed to pass wordlessly between them. Jem was sure Michaela's cheeks had suddenly flooded with rosy life. Their grip on each other became clammy. The counselor let go and practically leapt from her chair, as if she'd been stung.

"You get up when you feel ready," she said, busying herself with collecting the flannel and her book. "Everybody's having lunch. It'd do you some good. Join us when you can."

Jem watched as Michaela hurried into her room and felt her heart hammering in her chest.

The figure.

The memory of the figure by the lake was like a punch to the gut.

Somebody had been watching them. Was it the same somebody who had kidnapped Tommy? And Toombs?

Jem lay back down, the thoughts weighing heavily. Had she imagined the whole thing? The heat had been unbearable, and she was already paranoid about Tommy's disappearance. Could she have hallucinated the figure by the lake?

There was no way of knowing. All she knew was that something horrible was happening at Camp Genesis, and it was about time she figured out what.

● ● ●

Kyle cut his thumb and swore.

"Watch your mouth, dickweed," Donny said, slapping Kyle's head.

"I cut myself."

"Potato peeler didn't draw blood, so get back to work." Donny grabbed a pile of peeled potatoes and started slicing them by the stove.

Billy scratched his arm but he didn't say anything, going back to peeling his own pile.

After lunch, the younger campers got to go swimming while the other cabins were split into cleaning and cooking. The girls, except for drama queen Jem, had to bake and sweep while the boys had rough kitchen duty and manlier tasks like cleaning the gutters.

Kyle had tried getting paired with Neal but no such luck. Glen had ordered Neal to stick around for a one-on-one counselling session while Kyle and Billy of all people had to help scumbag Donny prep for dinner.

"Can't we prep rice instead of potatoes?" Kyle asked.

"Rice doesn't need any prep," Billy said. "You just throw it in boiling water."

"Thanks, Julia Childs." Kyle snickered and scraped off more potato skin.

"Pillow biters, hey, little less chatting, little faster peeling, okay?" Donny said, his knife flashing across the cutting board.

"Does Katherine let you talk like that?" Billy asked coldly.

"Katherine ain't here."

"But she's got eyes and ears everywhere," Billy said.

"Yeah, well…" Donny trailed off.

Kyle couldn't help but smirk. He never would have thought wallflower Billy would put Donny in his place. He couldn't imagine anyone coming to work in Camp Genesis unless they were delusional or out of all other options. Was the head cook scared to lose the little power he had accrued this summer?

As soon as Kyle finished his pile of potatoes, he left to go to the bathroom before Donny could give him another task. He decided to take his time and go to the bathroom all the way back in their cabin.

On the way, he spotted Neal and Glen sitting on a bench by the water.

It would be wrong to sneak over there and eavesdrop.

Kyle snuck up to a tree behind the bench where he could hear the conversation but stay hidden.

"You're from around here, right?" Glen asked.

"Yeah, not too far."

"So you must be a big Broncos fan, huh? I love them, when they're not playing Green Bay, I mean."

Ugh, what are they even talking about? This isn't juicy.

Kyle fought the urge to leave, leaning against the tree.

"Yeah, they're all right. I'm more into baseball," Neal said. "Not like Colorado's ever going to have a national baseball team, though."

"See, this is the cool young man I like talking to," Glen said. "No brooding. Nothing queer. Just two guys talking. Between you and me, I don't even care all that much about gays. I mean, don't hit on me and I'll leave you alone, you know? But this is a job. So let's see if I can't get some counseling in."

"I'm the last guy here who needs any counseling. Start with one of the other guys."

"Like Kyle?" Glen asked. "He's a lost case."

I'll take that as a compliment.

"At least he came back to give it another shot," Neal said. "I can respect that."

"That's because of what you and I have in common," Glen said. "We're both perfectionists. But you need to take a lesson from Kyle. It's ok to stumble, just as long as you don't give up."

Not exactly the lesson I'd like to teach Neal.

"What if…what if I didn't really fall but it just looks like it?" Neal finally asked.

"Never too late. Why don't you tell me about it?"

Neal stared at the ground for a bit.

"We were playing seven minutes in heaven."

"Where you're locked in a cupboard with a girl and make out?" Glen asked.

Neal nodded. "The guys thought it'd be funny to lock me in

with another dude. I got confused...I thought I was in there with a girl. We kissed, but I didn't mean it. I was confused."

Sure you were, Neal.

Kyle sort of felt sorry for him. Kyle had always been confident in his sexuality. Maybe it was because he had so many siblings. Nobody really cared what he did; he got lost in the mix. Anything that made him stand out was only a good thing. His parents disagreed.

"Let me guess. The guys opened the cupboard and found you making out with the dude," Glen said.

Neal's fists were clenched and Kyle thought he saw tears rolling down his cheeks.

"I was confused," he said. "I didn't mean it."

Glen sighed and cleaned his Coke-bottle glasses with his shirt. "I'm glad you felt able to share that with me, Neal. It takes a lot of bravery and it's the first step on the road to recovery."

"I just want to be normal."

"And we're here to help you. All you have to do is let us. Pray with me?"

Neal nodded, his gaze still fixed on the ground.

Glen began reciting a prayer and Kyle decided it was time to bail out. He hurried back to the kitchen, hoping he hadn't been gone too long, and realized he finally had something over Billy– he'd seen Neal fragile, and he could use that to help him win Neal over.

Chapter 12

When the guys returned to their cabin after mess hall chores, Glen gave each of them a granola bar and a bottle of water. Billy pressed the cool bottle to the back of his neck and sighed. Today was a scorcher; no wonder Jem had fainted. He'd never seen anybody pass out before and he felt a surge of pride that he'd managed to catch her just before she cracked her skull open on the stage.

Maybe there's a little He-Man in me after all.

He wished the counselors would let him check in on her, but Michaela said Jem needed her rest. The way Michaela said it she obviously thought there was something going on between him and Jem. She seemed pleased. Billy wondered what was wrong with just being friends. As far as he could tell, you could never have too many of those.

"What are these for?" Matthew asked, already unwrapping the granola bar and shoving it into his mouth.

"Time for a hike," Glen announced. He was sweating heavily and reminded Billy of a big, hairless hog.

"Cool," Neal said before gulping the water down in one swig.

He's so awesome.

"Yeah, cool. But only if I get to hike my skirt up," Kyle joked.

Rolling his eyes, Billy said, "Is hiking such a good idea? I mean, Jem just passed out from the heat."

"Don't be a sissy," Glen said. He wafted air under his sweaty armpits, then seemed to realize how feminine that looked and quickly stopped, clearing his throat and beating his chest as if something was lodged there.

"You'll be fine." Neal slapped Billy on the back.

"Okay."

Kyle glared at Billy.

After their shower incident, Billy liked Kyle even less. He was a snake, and he'd do anything to get what he wanted. Billy decided he'd make that as difficult for Kyle as possible.

If I can't have Neal, neither can Kyle.

The thought surprised him. What happened to push-over Billy? The one who always fell in line and never ruffled feathers?

Guess I never had anything worth fighting for before.

"You boys report to Father Oliver's cabin. He's taking you," Glen said. He was already on his second granola bar.

"You're not coming?" Steven asked.

"Nope."

"Yeah," Brady said, unleashing his lopsided grin with full force. "Glen needs to take a break. He only gets five a day."

"Out, wise guy," Glen said, pointing toward the door.

Billy trundled after the others, out into the sunny afternoon and toward Father Oliver's cabin. Cobb was already sweating.

Father Oliver met them on the path. The priest looked like Paul Bunyan in khaki shorts, showing off salt and pepper leg hair, and a short sleeve plaid shirt. His silver cross dangled from his neck, and his thumbs hooked around the straps of his backpack. Billy hoped it was filled with more water bottles.

"Ready for some fun, boys?"

"Yeah, when's it start?" Matthew grumbled.

"Now, now," Father Oliver chided him.

"Is Jem all right?" Billy asked.

"I've been assured she is perfectly fine. Merely a little overheated from that dress. Katherine told me to mention to you boys that's one of the evils of wearing dresses."

"Couldn't catch me dead in a dress," Neal said.

"But you have the legs for it," Brady joked. Only Cobb laughed with him.

Without looking at him, Neal gave Brady a one-handed shove that sent the goofy stoner stumbling into Cobb.

"All right, time we should be going," Father Oliver said. He led the way toward the path in the woods, with the guys falling in line behind him.

Billy and the others entered the woods in a tight group, but as the minutes ticked by, some fell behind and the cluster turned into a long line with Father Oliver at the front and Cobb far behind. Even in the shade of the trees the heat was unbearable. Billy wasn't a fan of going shirtless, but the urge to tear his T-shirt off his sweaty back grew with every step. He felt bad for Cobb and considered walking with him, but then he realized Kyle was right at Neal's side shortly behind Father Oliver.

I'm not letting him show me up.

Billy hurried away from Brady, in mid joke, and pushed himself until he caught up with the others, walking on Neal's free side.

"What's up?" he asked.

"Walking," Neal said with a friendly grin. "You?"

"Same. Walk is good." He rolled his eyes. *Sound cool, just one time!*

"You don't think you're going to faint like your girlfriend?" Kyle said.

"You wish. And Jem's not my girlfriend."

"Too bad. You two are cute together." Neal grinned at him, and Billy felt butterflies again.

"Do you have a girlfriend?" he asked. Maybe it was best to play into Neal's denial issues.

"Naw. I don't like getting tied down to just one girl."

"Cool." Billy gave Kyle a winning look. The blond boy just

squinted back at him.

Father Oliver stopped abruptly once they reached the small clearing where they'd had their first campfire. Billy had no idea how long they'd been walking, realizing that Father Oliver had taken them the long way there, but relief washed over him as he sat on one of the stumps.

He glanced around at the other guys, relieved to see that they were all sweating as badly as him.

Seven panting, sweaty gay guys alone in the woods with a priest. Sounds like a really bad joke.

"Looks like we made it in one piece," Father Oliver beamed. The heat didn't seem to be fazing him as much as the others. Billy wondered what his secret was. Prayer?

The priest sat down and set his backpack by his feet. "Water and granola time, guys."

Billy was done with his refreshments by the time Cobb finally reached them, his face and shirt drenched.

"Glad to see you here," Father Oliver greeted Cobb, who managed to grunt something back and practically collapse on a stump. "Relax and enjoy your granola bar and water."

"Already did," Cobb said.

Father Oliver unzipped his backpack and tossed Cobb another bottle of water.

"Thanks."

"Anyone else still thirsty?"

Billy wanted to raise his hand with Brady and Steven, but he didn't want to look weak in front of Neal.

"One guarantee I can make," Father Oliver said, "no one's having any sinful thoughts while hiking."

Not exactly true.

"Exercise is a great way to occupy your mind," Neal said.

"Exactly my point. If idle hands are the devil's playthings, then idle minds are the devil's video games."

Was that Neal's trick? Billy supposed they all had their own way of distracting themselves from their "unhealthy" desires. Video games and movies were Billy's escape. They helped him forget. Did Neal do the same with sports?

"That's trippy," Brady said. "But what does the Devil do while we're playing video games?"

"I'm afraid that's the end of the metaphor," Father Oliver said. He reached into his backpack and took out a handful of folded pages. "I want to share with you some testimonials from prior campers. These are all success stories that I hope will shed some light on why it is we're trying to help you."

"Oh yeah," Kyle said as the priest handed out the paper. "Katherine made everyone write letters at the end of the summer."

And all she has to show are eight success stories? And how many failures?

Billy took his letter and unfolded it. It felt so bizarre to read another gay kid's writing.

Before Camp Genesis, I was really depressed. I thought about killing myself all the time, but I knew that was a sin. But so were my thoughts. I didn't know what to do. I wished a bus could run me over and spare my family the shame.

I was scared at first to come to camp, but Katherine and the counselors were really terrific. We talked everything out, and I learned how to think differently. Now I don't want to die so bad. Now I want a girlfriend and kids, and I can't wait to go back home and show everyone how much I've changed.

Camp Genesis saved my life.

Billy reread the letter, moved by the raw emotion and plight of the stranger. He wanted to know how the guy was doing and if he still felt like that. The other campers were quiet as they read their letters until Kyle started laughing.

"What's so funny?" Neal asked. "These are serious."

"Yeah, I don't think this one's a success story," Kyle said.

"And why is that?" Father Oliver asked.

"'Cause this one's the letter I wrote last year."

"Congratulations, Mr. Majors, you've just nominated yourself as our topic of discussion for the afternoon."

Great, put even more attention on Kyle.

For the first time since camp started, Kyle looked nervous. As Father Oliver stared unblinkingly at him, Kyle's usual eyebrow-arching arrogance drooped into a frown.

"Er, huh?"

Billy looked at the priest. What was he up to?

"Stand at the center of the group, please," Father Oliver said. "And Billy, pass these along. Everybody take two pieces of paper."

The priest handed Billy a handful of blank sheets of paper and some pencils. He took some paper and passed the rest to Neal at his side, who passed the stationery on around the circle.

Kyle stood at the center of the clearing, wafting his T-shirt to circulate the air against his taut stomach.

Jerk.

"Is it time for figure drawing? How do you want me to pose?" he asked.

"There'll be no talking from now on," Father Oliver said sternly. Billy was surprised. The priest was normally so friendly, but he wasn't smiling anymore. "Now, everybody, you all know Kyle. What I want you to do is write down a single adjective describing him. Give him a good look and come up with the best adjective you can think of. And, please, keep it PG."

Kyle's jaw ticked ever so slightly. For once, he didn't look like he enjoyed being the center of attention. Did Kyle actually care what people thought of him? He usually seemed so confident.

Confident.

Billy wrote that down on his scrap of paper. It would be simple to write something mean and he wanted to go with the priest's game. Sometimes conforming was just easier.

"Everybody done?" Father Oliver said. "All right, pass them along."

Billy collected the paper and handed it all to the priest. Father Oliver flipped through them one at a time, pondering the words. He pocketed two of them with a sigh.

"I did say keep it PG," he said as Cobb and Brady shoved each other and laughed. The priest fixed them with a long, hard stare until they blushed and fell silent. Billy suddenly felt uneasy. He wasn't Kyle's biggest fan, but this was a pretty humiliating exercise—he didn't imagine any of the adjectives the others had picked would be particularly generous.

And he'd never imagined Father Oliver could be so cold.

"Right, the first card," the priest said, holding it up. "'Athletic.' That's a good one."

Kyle flexed and bowed.

"Next, 'Arrogant.' Interesting."

Was that hurt in Kyle's eyes? Billy tried not to feel bad for him. He brought this sort of stuff on himself. And it was true.

"And this one says 'Mean.'"

Kyle glanced down at his feet, but he remained silent.

"Finally, 'Confident.' Very good." Father Oliver handed the bits of paper to Kyle. "There you go," he said. "Now, wasn't that interesting? Not a single one of you wrote down the word 'homosexual.'"

"That's sort of a given," Brady said.

"Nevertheless, it wasn't a word that any of you chose as the most important adjective to describe Kyle."

Where's this going?

"You see, you're so blind to that fact that you don't regard it as important—but it's the very reason you're at Camp Genesis.

Homosexuality is not something to trivialize or ignore. Ignoring it can be very dangerous. These feelings you're all having, they're dangerous. You've all made brave first steps by attending camp. You're acknowledging those sinful feelings, confronting them, and we're going to help absolve you of them."

Billy felt sick. Up until then, he'd seen Father Oliver as a benevolent ally. He was cheerful and open and seemed to like everybody. Billy saw that there was more to it than that. The priest really did believe that they were living in sin and needed to be saved.

"Kyle, you may sit down."

"What did you assholes write about me?" Kyle asked Cobb and Brady as he sat between them.

"There is to be no talking," Father Oliver reminded them. "Okay, next task. I want you all to think of something somebody has said to you that made you feel bad. It can be from any time in your life, but it has to be true and it has to have hurt. The more honest you are, the better. Remember, this is all confidential."

Billy looked down at his blank piece of paper. Why was Father Oliver asking them to do this? Was it really going to help them? Make them feel better? Cure them?

He found himself thinking about a time he'd been walking home from school, and he passed a group of guys. They were from a different high school, but he recognized them from his neighborhood. They all jeered at him as he went by, and one of them yelled, "Hey, skinny kid, off to shove your finger up your ass?"

He couldn't write that. Could he? It had definitely hurt. He'd been stunned at first. Felt hot and numb at the same time. When he got home, he cried in his room for an hour.

His heart thumping, Billy wrote the insult down and folded the paper over so he didn't have to look at it. He peered at the other guys, who all looked as miserable as he felt. The clearing in the woods was oddly quiet.

"Everybody done?" Father Oliver asked. He went around the group and collected the bits of paper. He then redistributed them at random, handing two pieces to Billy and none to Kyle.

"Kyle, stand up again, please," the priest said.

Looking sceptical, Kyle returned to the center of the group.

"Now, I want you all, one at a time, to read what's on your bits of paper, but direct it at Kyle."

Billy couldn't believe his ears. The priest wanted them to hurl insults at one of their fellow campers?

This is ridiculous!

"Trust me," the priest said, apparently reading their shock. "It's all part of the exercise. Cobb, you go first."

Cobb looked at his paper nervously and cleared his throat. "You're..." he started. He glanced at Kyle, then Father Oliver, then back at his paper. "You're a fucking faggot, and you deserve to rot in Hell," he said quietly.

Father Oliver's face betrayed no emotion.

"Steven," he prompted.

Steven looked just as awkward as Cobb. "Pretty boys like you are born dick-less," he said, not looking at Kyle.

It looked like Kyle wanted to laugh. Or cry. Billy couldn't be sure.

"Get a bra; you got bigger tits than my sister," Neal said. Billy forced himself not to glance at Cobb.

"If your queer ass even looks at me in the shower, then I'm going to kill you," Matthew said miserably.

"This is stupid," Brady said.

"Follow my directions, or you'll miss out on the overnight camping trip."

Brady sighed and said, "You're a sissy faggot nigger."

The campers turned toward Steven, but no one said anything.

Billy stared down at his two bits of paper. One of them must be his; nobody else had read it.

"Father," he said, looking at the priest. "I can't—"

"Go ahead, William," Father Oliver said in an emotionless voice. "Read them."

Wrestling with his conscience, Billy stared at Kyle, who stared back at him. His eyes had gone glassy and he was pale. His jaw was clenched, as if he were holding back tears.

"Just do it," Kyle said.

"Hey, skinny kid," Billy said, tears springing to his eyes, both at the memory and the humiliation and because of Kyle's face. "Off to shove your finger up your ass?" He shared a look with Kyle. They were both crying. He just had to read the final one.

Do it quickly.

"You're a fucking moron and you always will be."

Tears streamed down his cheeks. He couldn't bring himself to look at Kyle, but he heard a sniffle at the center of the clearing.

"Very good," Father Oliver said. "It seems you've all experienced bullying, and now you've experienced being a bully. Neither is healthy."

The quiet was deafening.

Billy hated him.

"Father," Brady said. "What was the point of that?"

"Nobody wants to live their lives being persecuted," the priest said. "You can be sure, though, that if you give in to your unhealthy desires, you will be persecuted for the rest of your lives. You will be subject to insults like those and much worse."

None of the campers said a word. Billy couldn't make eye contact with any of them. Kyle quietly sat back down.

Father Oliver grinned at them, his eyes twinkling again. "Well then, that's enough tough love for the moment. You scamps relax here while I bring the ladies out for some fun improvisation exercises. I think you're really going to enjoy those."

● ● ●

Michaela left the cabin after she set the girls up playing puzzles and board games. She needed a breather. Jem was going to be fine after her fainting spell, but Michaela still found herself worrying about her more than the other girls combined.

Not just worrying, but thinking about Jem in general.

She strolled along the beach until she found herself padding up to Katherine's office.

Why'd I come here?

She knocked on the door and waited. Maybe Katherine wouldn't even be there. But then she'd have to come up with some other excuse to stay away from the cabin.

"Door's open!"

Michaela entered and found Katherine looking over paperwork.

"How's the girl doing?" Katherine asked.

"She's just fine."

"Great to hear." Katherine set the paper down, smiling. "We may have to rethink some of the outdoors exercises. I'd hate for another child to pass out again."

"Good idea." Michaela shuffled her feet. It was strange how just being in Katherine's presence made her feel more clear-headed. She could see Jem through Katherine's eyes, as a troubled young woman in need of help. Not somebody to moon over. Katherine's certainty was infectious. It was the reason Michaela always found herself at Katherine's office whenever wrong thoughts began trickling back into her head.

Katherine played with her wedding ring. "Is there anything else, Michaela?"

"I guess not." She didn't move.

"I'm most proud of you," Katherine said softly. "You are my greatest success story. I pray the girls will follow your lead."

"Thanks." Michaela considered leaving, but found herself asking a question. "Do you ever think we're too harsh on them?"

"The campers?" Michaela nodded and Katherine sighed. "To be honest, sometimes I think we are. But we're helping them; you're proof of that. The ones who see sense always write to me thanking me. They send photos of their partners and they're happy."

Michaela was surprised at the sad light in Katherine's eyes. There seemed to be more to it than that. Regret, maybe. Katherine had her own troubled past.

"I'm sure they'd be proud of what you've accomplished," Michaela said.

"Thank you." Katherine's voice held none of its usual brittleness.

"Well, I should get back to the girls."

Katherine nodded, returning to her paperwork.

Michaela shut the office door behind her and made her way between the cabins. Seeing Katherine was exactly what she'd needed. Finding the girls still playing board games, she made sure to give all of them her equal attention.

Chapter 13

After Father Oliver's exercise, the campers made their way back to camp. Billy saw Kyle hurrying off ahead of everyone and broke into a jog to catch up with him.

"Hey, Kyle—"

"Back off, nerd."

Kyle picked up his pace, and Billy double-timed to keep up. He was pretty sure Kyle was still crying, or at least trying to hold the tears in until he could shut himself in the cabin bathroom.

"I wanted to say—" he panted.

"If you say 'sorry' I'll knock your teeth out," Kyle snapped.

Billy didn't doubt that for a second, especially not after what Kyle just went through. He couldn't give up, though. Kyle had been really hurt, and Billy was tired of the scathing looks Kyle always gave him.

"I'm—"

Kyle spun to face him. "You enjoyed it, admit it. You enjoyed doing that."

"What? No, I—"

"Nobody else sees what a whining little brat you are, but I do." Kyle's face was beet red and his knuckles were bone white as he gripped his backpack straps.

Billy knew Kyle was lashing out, but he couldn't help yelling back.

"You're pissed at the wrong people! I don't care if you're gay, straight, back-to-front, have a weird obsession with cats. *They* do. *They're* the ones trying to change us."

For a second, it seemed Kyle was actually listening. Then his expression hardened.

"Just stay away from me." He turned and hurried off toward camp.

Billy's shoulders slumped and he trudged after. Kyle seemed to have hated him on sight, and there was nothing he could say to change that. Billy hadn't cared about Kyle before, writing him off as snippy and self-important. Today's activity had changed that. There was pain there, and Billy had finally glimpsed the face Kyle always hid from the world. Maybe they'd never be friends, but he wanted to try to make him feel better.

"He'll come around." Brady appeared at his side.

"I dunno, he's pretty mad. And he should be."

"This place is getting worse," Brady said.

"Didn't think that was possible."

• • •

Kyle ate dinner on Neal's left side while Billy chatted quietly on his right. Glen barely touched his meal before leaving the guys to chat with Donny. Cobb plowed through his food and then got a second helping. Kyle barely touched his, just twirled his fork in his mashed potatoes. He formed the sloppy mess into a frowning face while the others compared their favorite actors from *Doctor Who*. Again.

He was still pissed about the activity in the woods. How dare Father Oliver single him out like that? And who did these guys think they were, calling him arrogant and bitchy? He was sure Brady and Cobb had called him a slut, or some derivative. *Screw them all.*

Except maybe Neal. Was he the one that wrote "athletic?"

"Do you watch *Doctor Who*, Kyle?"

Kyle snapped to at the mention of his own name. It was Neal, apparently trying to bring him into the conversation. He probably felt bad about the exercise, too.

Kyle looked up at him with a forced grin and realized Neal was staring at his frowny food sculpture.

"Uh. No, I have friends," Kyle said.

Neal cracked a grin and Brady giggled, but the others went silent.

Glen returned to the table and hovered over the guys. "You 'bout done with everything?" They chorused that they were. "Good. So tonight's going to be a little different than usual. Father Oliver wants to check in with Kyle to, uh, see how he's doing, um, compared to last year. Anyway, I'm going to go with him, which means the rest of you get a free night in the cabin. I don't want you getting into any trouble. Stay put, play board games, listen to music at a reasonable volume. And I'm putting Billy and Neal in charge."

Yeah, pair them up. Thanks, dickhead.

"You can count on us," Neal told him, slapping Billy's back.

You're killing me here.

Kyle stabbed his mashed potato face and stood up from the table. "All right, let's get this over with." The guys waved goodbye as he trotted away with Glen. As they left the mess hall, he asked, "How long is this therapy session going to last?"

"You're not going to therapy," Glen said. "I know you can keep a secret, right?"

Kyle nearly stopped in his tracks. "Are you going to hit on me? 'Cause last year—"

"Don't be stupid, kid. I'm hooking up with Lisa. And I'm an anti-gay counselor, remember?"

"I remember last year when—"

"Can it. You can keep a secret, right?"

"Sure I can. Go on."

Glen led Kyle toward Father Oliver's cabin as he explained,

"Norton Toombs took off the other day. He was our fifth. So now we need a new fifth."

"Fifth for what?" Kyle asked.

"You'll see."

Kyle hurried after Glen as they neared Father Oliver's cabin. Glen opened the door and Kyle's jaw dropped. A large round table had been set up with a green felt cover. There were poker chips, playing cards, and cigars laid out. Father Oliver, wearing plaid, placed a fifth chair around the table as they entered.

"Shut the door," Father Oliver said. "Kyle, are you game?"

"Christ yes. I mean, er, just yes, Father." Kyle took a seat. After the group therapy session in the woods, he felt uneasy around Father Oliver. "Who else is playing? Anybody good?"

"The three of us, Michaela, and Donny the cook," Glen said as he took a seat. "We're the 'cool kids.' Poker's no good without five players, and I thought you would be fun to play with."

"I'm honored," Kyle said with a smirk.

"You beat out Brady in a coin toss," Father Oliver said with a wink.

Glen continued his spiel. "And like I said, this is a secret. We play every few days or so. Don't say anything to the others, and you can keep your seat at the table."

"Nice. Um, no offense, but do priests gamble?"

Father Oliver chuckled and sat down next to him. "Strictly speaking, it's not gambling if it's a game of skill, which I happen to excel at. And we only play for quarters. I'd never condone high stakes gaming."

"Oh. I don't have any quarters."

"I'm covering you this time," Glen said. "But if you win, I get half the pot."

"Deal."

"You know how to play Texas Hold 'Em?" Glen asked him.

"Oh, I may have played once or twice before," Kyle said. No

need to let them know he'd made a couple hundred bucks over the school year playing with the seniors after school. He'd also convinced some of them to play strip poker, which was always a blast.

Father Oliver started shuffling a well-worn deck when the door opened and Michaela entered. "Hey, guys. So I see you replaced Norton already. And with a camper?"

"I have seniority," Kyle boasted.

Michaela frowned but didn't say anything else. She sat next to Father Oliver and pulled out a rolled stack of quarters from her jacket pocket.

"You're organized tonight," Glen said.

"My laundry money." Michaela set the roll in a clay jar that looked like it had been made by a camper, and then started placing chips in front of each seat. Glen put a ten in the jar, and Father Oliver placed a five dollar bill. Kyle noticed the name "Miles C" carved into the clay bowl.

By the time the chips were distributed and Glen lit up his cigar, the door opened and Donny the cook entered.

"Hey boys…and Kyle," Donny said. The auburn-haired camp kitchen supervisor wore a denim shirt with the sleeves ripped off, revealing a grisly tattoo of an eagle catching a fish on one bicep. He held up a bottle of whiskey and set it on the table, then placed five singles in the money jar.

"All right," Kyle said, grabbing the bottle.

"Not you," Michaela said, placing a hand on his forearm.

"I'm old enough to join the army!"

"You could if you weren't a sissy," Donny teased.

"Which we're trying to cure," Glen said. Father Oliver shook his head and left the table.

"So that I can die in the army?" Kyle asked.

"There's no fighting going on," Michaela said.

"We're at war with Russia," Kyle stated. "Aren't we? Really, are we? I'm not sure."

Father Oliver returned with five small glasses. He poured the whiskey into each one and said, "Jesus turned water into wine. I think an eighteen year old can be allowed to have a glass of whiskey with us. He's only a year shy of the drinking age in Colorado. Besides, the age limit was raised to combat drunk driving. I don't think Kyle here will be driving anywhere this evening."

Okay, so maybe Father Oliver isn't completely evil.

Michaela didn't object. Kyle nodded and asked, "So which cigar is mine?"

● ● ●

Michaela was the first to run out of chips, followed a few hands later by Glen. Michaela wished Father Oliver luck and then returned to her cabin, but Glen stayed on as dealer to smoke another cigar and cheer Kyle on since he still had money riding on Kyle's success.

Kyle played with a few of his chips on the table, trying to distract the others, but it didn't seem to work well, as Donny, and then Father Oliver won the next two hands. Kyle thought he was going out, until he got pocket queens and fought the urge to make a joke about them.

"Well, I'm all in," Kyle said, pushing his pile of chips in the center of the table.

"I call you," Donny said, matching his chips.

"Too rich for my blood," Father Oliver said.

"But you're winning," Kyle said. "You know you wanna."

"Oh, fine. It's just for fun, anyway." Father Oliver matched the others' chips.

Kyle licked his lips, praying neither of his opponents had

anything better than his queens. Glen flipped over the rest of the cards, and Kyle stood up, pumping his fists in the air.

"Oh yeah! Eat my shorts, losers!" He realized he was talking to a priest and the guy who prepared his food and quickly sat back down. He quietly raked in his chips.

"Nice job," Glen said, patting Kyle's back. "I might just make my money back on you."

"Thanks."

"At least this one might pay off his debts," Donny grumbled.

"What's that?" Glen asked.

"Norton owes me a nice chunk of change," Donny said. "The psycho didn't leave it for me when he took off. He's lucky I don't burn down his shack."

Father Oliver coughed into his hand and Kyle shrugged it off.

Donny was out three hands later, and stormed out of the cabin after calling Kyle a "sissy card shark."

"Okay, *padre*," Kyle said, sizing up his opponent, "down to you and me."

"Let's have another drink first," Father Oliver said. He poured whiskey in three glasses, but barely any in his own. Glen and Kyle eagerly grabbed their drinks.

Kyle raised his up and toasted, "To finding fun in unexpected places."

"Hear hear," Glen said. He took a swig and added, "Now turn my five dollar investment into thirteen fifty."

"I'm doing my best." Kyle took another drink and realized the room wasn't as steady as he thought it was before. He giggled and set his glass down. "Donny's not going to poison me, right?"

"I wouldn't worry about it too much," Glen said. "Although I wouldn't put it past him; he *is* an ex-con."

"What!" Kyle never liked Katherine with her brimstone attitude, but it never crossed his mind that she'd purposefully hire dangerous employees.

"Yeah, just drugs and assault. Katherine saves money hiring ex-cons and illegal immigrants as support staff," Glen said.

"And college kids for counselors," Father Oliver pointed out. "I'm here for free."

"You're here to shark me out of my rainy day fund," Glen snickered. He started dealing the cards to the two remaining players.

Kyle tried to focus on the game through the cigar smoke and whiskey haze, but his thoughts kept drifting back to the ex-cons around them.

Yeah, "Camp Carnage" is definitely accurate. The next few hands Glen dealt Kyle were pitiful, and he tried bluffing, but Father Oliver didn't fall for it. Kyle's chips slowly dwindled until Father Oliver was able to force him all in. In the end, Kyle lost the game to a pair of sevens.

"This blows," Kyle said.

"I'd tell you I'm sorry, but it wouldn't be true." Smiling, Father Oliver raked in the chips.

"All right, Kyle, time for you to get to bed," Glen said. "I'm going to finish my cigar here; you think you can make it back to the cabin all right?"

"Of course, captain," Kyle said, his voice slurring.

"Tell the others I want them in bed when you get there."

"Aye, aye." Kyle stood up and left the cabin, the others chatting and joking. He had to steady himself from the swaying room.

As he walked through the dark campground, Kyle wished he'd taken some of the booze with him to impress Neal.

Clydesdale Neal, yum.

Kyle heard footsteps behind him. He spun around, but didn't see any movement. Kyle stumbled and fell to the ground. He started to giggle, but then clasped his hands over his mouth. More footsteps.

Uh oh.

Kyle scrambled up to his feet and ducked around a tree, hugging close to it. He hoped he was invisible in the darkness. He closed his eyes and wished the person would walk by without noticing him.

Something tickled the back of Kyle's throat and he threw up with a loud gagging fit, white spots obscuring his vision.

"Kyle Majors!"

He spun around and found Katherine Creevey standing a few feet away with her hands on her hips.

Shit shit shit!

"Uh, hi, Kate. Nice night for a stroll."

Her nostrils flared and she grabbed him by the arm. "Are you drunk, young man?"

"I'd go with tipsy," he said, trying not to laugh.

"I hope your mopping skills have improved since last year."

"I doubt it," he said.

"No camping trip for you."

Kyle was about to argue with her, but he grabbed his stomach and threw up some more.

Chapter 14

Billy peeked around the corner of the cabin nervously. When he was sure the coast was clear, he turned back to Brady just in time to see him spark up the lighter and take a drag on the joint. Glen had put him and Neal in charge until he got back, and they'd played games and listened to music for a while, until Brady had pulled him outside.

"What is it?" Billy had asked.

"Your boyfriend can handle watching the other spazzes," Brady said.

"He's not my boyfriend," Billy said, blushing. Was he that obvious about how he felt about Neal? Did Neal know? He started panicking and wasn't sure if he wanted to hide in his bed or pull Neal into it.

"Let's smoke."

"No way."

"Jem will want to," Brady said. "Will you if she does?"

"I don't know. But she's not here, so it doesn't matter."

"I told her at dinner to sneak out after lights out," Brady said with a wink.

"Fine."

When Jem arrived, the three of them snuck around the side of the cabin.

We're going to get caught.

He couldn't help being skittish. Katherine terrified him. The thought of being yanked into her office made him break out in a cold sweat.

"Bill never met a rule he didn't like," Jem joked, taking the joint from Brady.

"Hey," Billy objected, but it was sort of true. It wasn't that he *liked* rules exactly, but he was terrified of the repercussions if he broke them. When he was seven, he took some money that had been sitting out on the desk in his friend's house. His mom found out and drove him back to apologize to his friend's mom. It had been humiliating, but it had done the trick. He could still remember the two women berating him, making him feel so horrible. Billy never did anything bad again.

Until his parents discovered he was gay. Except there wasn't a quick fix for that. It wasn't that they were closed minded, but they were doctors and AIDS was a big deal. Billy guessed they were just trying to protect him from AIDS Harry.

Funny how protecting him resembled punishing him.

"Hey, space cadet." Jem offered him the joint.

Billy shook his head.

"It won't kill you," she said.

"Naw, man, you'll feel like you can touch the stars." Brady's eyes were bloodshot, and he looked like he didn't have a care in the world. He put his arms out and spun around, staring up at the starry sky. "Twinkle, twinkle," he called, then giggled.

Jem passed the joint to Brady.

"You feeling better now, princess?" he asked her, wedging the joint between his lips. "I know they want you girls to all be damsels in distress, but you took it to a whole other level today."

Jem punched his arm, and Brady hooted with laughter.

"At least it got me out of that ridiculous play," she muttered. Then, more seriously, she added, "So, there's something I need to do." The smoke curled about her mysteriously.

"Aside from getting into Michaela's shorts?" Brady joked.

"I'm serious," Jem said, and Billy could see that she was. "There's some seriously weird shit happening around here, and I don't like being the pawn in a bad mystery novel."

"Any idea what she's talking about?" Brady asked Billy.

Billy shook his head.

"Something happened to Camp Genesis four years ago," Jem said, taking another drag. "The whole place burnt down. They never found out who did it, and it's my guess that whoever was responsible is the one who's turned kidnapper 'round here."

"Who? Tommy and Toombs? They're probably in Hawaii enjoying cocktails and a massage right now," Brady said, taking the joint. "Gee, I hope those crazy kids can make it work."

"Yeah, I'm thinking not," Jem said.

"So what are you going to do?" Billy asked.

Jem looked at him, her eyes glittering mischievously. "I'm going to hitch a ride into town and start asking questions. There must be a records office somewhere. I want to know everything there is to know about this hell-hole. Every dirty little secret. Every unsigned contract, every disgruntled ex-employee."

"If there's anything, it's in Katherine's office," Brady pointed out. "Billy, you heard what Kyle said. She's hiding something."

"Yeah, if we can believe Kyle." Guilt nagged at Billy as he recalled Father Oliver's exercise in the woods. He could barely look at Kyle all evening, even though the blond boy seemed to have shrugged it off. Billy hoped he wouldn't wake up in the morning with his eyebrows shaved off.

Jem took the joint from Brady and took a deep, contemplative drag. "Katherine's office it is, then."

The sound of laughter came from inside the cabin and Billy jumped.

"If anybody's a damsel in distress, it's Billy," Brady joked.

Even Billy couldn't disagree with that. But where was his knight in shining armor?

"Nawww," Jem cooed, crushing Billy in a hug. "We'll look after you, Billy boy; we'll slay the dragon for you. Now take this." She offered him the joint again.

Billy looked at it curiously. Sometimes he hated being the damsel. The square. The one everybody had to look after. He could be He-Man in his computer games, but never in real life. What was wrong with him? For once, maybe the risk was worth it. If somebody offered Joan Collins a toke in *Dallas*, she'd do it in a heartbeat and probably roll the next five. Sometimes he liked to fantasize that he and Joan were somehow related—they *did* have the same last name—and she'd whisk him away one day to a better life. Perhaps it was time to inject a little Joan Collins into his life.

Carpe Collins.

Seize the Collins.

Time to put his last name to good use.

He cast a doubtful look around and then took the joint.

He put it to his lips and prepared to inhale.

"William Collins!"

Billy's blood ran cold.

Katherine Creevey had appeared at the side of the cabin, her face taut with anger. She held Kyle's arm and shoved him toward the cabin door. "You, get to bed immediately."

"I don't so feel good," Kyle muttered as he swayed inside.

Katherine strode over to Billy and plucked the joint from his lips, her skeletal features pale. "You three. My office. Now."

Trembling, Billy stumbled after her. Jem and Brady walked along either side of him, but Billy refused to look at either of them. What was going to happen to them now? Images of the sex dungeon Kyle had mentioned leapt to his mind. Of Katherine stringing them up and whipping them. Ridiculous? The look on Katherine's face said otherwise.

Katherine flipped the light on as she entered her office. Her heels clipped across the hardwood floor, and her shoulders were tensed like a hungry lioness ready to pounce.

"Close the door."

Brady did as she said, and the three of them lined up as if they were in front of a firing squad.

"I needn't tell you how disappointed I am," Katherine said, her features bloodless. Billy couldn't look at her. He averted his gaze to the floor, feeling like a naughty schoolboy.

I am a naughty schoolboy.

Out of the corner of his vision, he saw her raise the joint before her like it was a poisonous dart.

"A marijuana cigarette!" She shook her head. "Contraband like this is strictly forbidden on camp grounds, not to mention illegal, as I'm sure you're all well aware. I don't suppose I need to ask who's responsible for bringing it into the camp."

"I am," Jem said.

"No! It was me," Brady said.

Billy looked at them in surprise. Did he have to throw himself on his sword, too? He hadn't even smoked any of it. Katherine had seen to that.

"I—" he started, but Katherine cut him off.

"Quiet, all of you," she snapped. "Regardless of who brought this filth into my camp, you're all responsible for conspiring to smoke it, and that can't go unpunished."

Billy noticed stuffed stag heads on the walls behind her. The way Katherine stood, their horns seemed to sprout from her own head. She looked demonic in her rage.

"You're all banned from the camping trip. While everybody's off having fun, you'll be here doing chores. Cleaning, repairing, earning your keep."

"What a crock," Jem muttered.

Katherine straightened like she'd been struck by lightning, and it seemed she was ready to erupt in an explosion of anger.

The knock at the door saved them.

"Yes?"

The word left Katherine's lips like a bullet.

Father Oliver appeared.

"Ah," he smiled pleasantly, before reading the atmosphere in the room. "Jemima, Brady, William."

"Father Oliver," Katherine said. "I'm afraid we have three more campers who'll be staying behind during the camping excursion."

The priest's face sagged. "Oh. That is distressing news. Might I ask why?"

"They've broken camp regulations—not to mention the law." She held up the joint with a look of disgust. Without warning, she flung it into the fireplace. Brady sighed deeply. "They'll stay behind for chore duty."

"Are you sure—"

Katherine raised a hand. "I've made my decision," she said with a suffocating finality. She looked at Billy and the others. "Get out of my sight."

Shame ringing in his ears, Billy went to the door. Brady and Jem left before him. As he closed the door behind him, he heard Father Oliver speak up.

"Katherine, are you sure it's wise to separate the campers like this? Especially given the current situation with Tommy and Norton?"

Billy closed the door.

He couldn't help agreeing with the priest.

Chapter 15

Michaela woke feeling optimistic. Some mornings were worse than others, but on that Thursday, she felt ready to take on the world. Of all her campers, only one wouldn't be allowed to go on the overnight camping trip with them. As mischievous as teenagers were, she figured that keeping seven of eight out of trouble was a pretty good percentage.

After straightening out her bed and making sure her striped pajamas were on straight, Michaela entered the main cabin. Her girls slept soundly, some snoring, some mumbling, and others looking dead to the world.

Michaela planted her hands on her hips and shouted, "Good morning, ladies!" Most of the girls stirred, a few of them grumbling. "We're scheduled to eat breakfast in forty-five minutes. So the shower line needs to start. After that, we have a few activities with the other girls' cabin, and don't forget the camping trip tonight. We're leaving after lunch."

"How could I forget it?" Jem asked.

"Everyone else, remember, you still need to behave yourselves; otherwise, you'll have to stay back here and do chores with Jem and the boys. Sorry, Jem." As bad as Michaela felt, she could at least use Jem as a warning to the others. And there was that part, back deep in her mind, that knew it would be best that she didn't sleep under the stars with Jem.

"Which boys are staying back?" Nikki asked.

"That doesn't matter," Michaela said. *Wait, that* should *matter. Is Nikki interested in one of them? Am I getting through to her? Finally!*

"Why not?" Nikki asked.

"Because plenty more boys will be with us on the trip than scrubbing the floors. Sorry, again, Jem."

Jem just patted her messy, purple bedhead and started gathering her clothes. Michaela took that as a respectful enough sign and returned to her private room to get ready for the day; it was sure to be a long one.

Michaela was so anxious about the trip, she managed to get her girls to the mess hall ten minutes ahead of schedule. Glen was already there with his boys in tow.

What a show off.

"All right, girls, looks like Donny's putting the food out now. As soon as he's ready, line up."

Michaela's sleep-deprived girls nodded and sat at one of the tables, some of them resting their heads on the chipped table top. Michaela found Katherine sitting in a corner, speaking with Father Oliver and Glen. She left her girls and joined the adults.

"Good morning," Michaela said, sounding even more chipper than she felt.

"Top of the morning," Father Oliver said.

"Michaela, I'm so glad to see you," Katherine said.

"Oh?"

"I was planning on telling you after lunch, but now's as good a time as any." Katherine paused, and Michaela fought the urge to ask her to get on with it. "I think it would be helpful to have Glen on the trip with us, since he has more outdoors experience, and it appears that the boys staying here don't listen to him."

"I don't know what the problem is," Glen said, affecting a sheep dog frown that Michaela assumed was an act.

"Okay," Michaela said. "Who's staying with the trouble-makers then?"

Katherine coughed into her hand and said, "It looks like

Donny, Father Oliver, and, well, you." She must have spotted the disappointment on Michaela's face, as she added, "I need someone responsible to help Father Oliver with the boys, and you know Donny's only purview is the kitchen. You're my most reliable counselor."

"That's nice of you to say, but—"

"Yeah, you're great. A real role model for me," Glen added, cutting her off.

Slimy worm.

"I still have my reservations about this trip," Father Oliver stated. "I'd like to postpone it at least a day. We need to track down Norton and Tommy."

"Still no word from them?" Michaela asked.

"I'm sure they're fine," Katherine said. "I'll make a call into the police department and see if Norton's washed up yet."

"Let me know what you find," Father Oliver said as Katherine left the table.

"I'm starving," Glen said. "See you later." He hopped up and hurried to the front of the line as it formed in front of Donny.

Father Oliver shared a quick smile with Michaela and said, "Looks like we're chaperoning tonight, my dear. We'll make sure the kids get their chores done early, and then we can have our own misfit campfire and sing along."

"That would be nice. But are you really worried something's happened to Norton and Tommy?"

"Yes, I'm afraid I am."

● ● ●

After lunch, Jem sat at the window of Cabin Two and watched the other campers congregate in the sunshine. There were about twenty-five of them, all wearing bright red baseball caps and backpacks, rolled-up sleeping bags under their arms. The younger kids shrieked and chased each other. The older ones pretended they weren't checking each other out behind their shades.

Lucky fags.

She'd never had good luck. Getting banned from the trip was just another unsurprisingly lame development in her increasingly lame life.

Bright side? Katherine's heading into the woods with the kids. Her office will be empty.

Jem smiled deviously to herself. She couldn't imagine Katherine camping. She pictured the camp owner lining a load of beauty creams up inside her tent while wearing a hair net.

That said, Katherine was from Texas, so she figured she had a revolver stowed in each boot for putting down rabid squirrels.

Or unruly campers.

Outside, Katherine clapped her hands and Counselor Lisa blew her whistle. Katherine said something Jem couldn't hear, then turned and strutted toward the lake. The counselors and campers followed behind, marching like a pack of little soldiers.

Jem gave it thirty minutes, each one ticking painfully by. That should leave her enough time to break into Katherine's office, do a little Nancy Drew-ing, and still make it out in time to meet the others and receive chore instructions from Father Oliver.

She left the cabin and went around the back. Best to stay out of sight. She skirted along the back of the cabins and it wasn't long before she reached Katherine's office.

Jem peered around the corner of the cabin. Neal and Steven were tossing a football back and forth on the far side of the camp.

Isn't Steven supposed to be off on the camping trip?

Realizing that she was wasting time, Jem sized up the distance from where she stood to the office door. If she moved fast, they wouldn't spot her.

I'm screwed if the door's locked.

Refusing to let that thought stop her, she dashed quickly up the steps to the office door and pushed it open. She shut the door quickly, feeling like her heart was in her throat.

Katherine, you're far too trusting.

Knowing she didn't have much time, Jem looked around the office. Where to start?

She went straight to the desk and went through all of the drawers. There were papers, but nothing important. Bills and personal notes. There were papers on the desktop, too, but they were all unbelievably boring.

Next: the filing cabinet.

Jem pulled open the top drawer and flipped quickly through the files. There were labels with years marked up on them, and files with campers' names. She dreaded to think what her own file said.

The second drawer was for staff. Intrigued, Jem pulled open the file on Norton Toombs. Vietnam vet, just as the girls in her cabin had said. History of drug abuse. Mother lived somewhere out of state. Psychiatric analysis: pending.

Jem frowned. She was sure there were loads of hoops people had to jump through before they were allowed to work with kids. According to Toombs' file, though, he'd never seen a single one of those hoops.

What kind of camp is Katherine running here?

She pulled another file: Donny Campbell, the cook. High-school dropout. History of drug abuse. Three arrests, all for arson. No family apart from a sister.

Unnerved, Jem replaced the file. She stopped. Right at the back, almost as if it had been forgotten, rested a file that looked older.

Brian Creevey.

Jem pulled it out. It had been ripped into quarters and then taped back together. According to the file, Brian was forty-one, an upstanding citizen, attended the Texas State Technical College.

Then Jem found the death certificate.

Cause of death: strangling.

Next of kin: Katherine Creevey.

Was this Katherine's husband?

Jem froze.

Somebody walked up the steps to the office. Jem slid the file back into the cabinet and searched for somewhere to hide, but there was no back to Katherine's desk and no other furniture big enough to conceal her.

She noticed another door to what might be a closet and dashed quickly to it. Yanking the door open, she found a medium-sized bathroom with shiny silver fittings.

Neat.

The office door opened and Jem threw herself into the bathroom. Without a second to spare, she drew the door closed without shutting it—the click would alert the newcomer to her presence.

Footsteps traipsed over the floorboards. Not heavy but not light, either.

Who could it be?

Jem's heart hammered against her ribs. Whoever it was, they were moving about the office casually.

She heard the phone being picked up and dialled.

"It's me," a voice said.

She recognized it immediately.

Holding her breath, Jem eased into the gap between the door and the frame.

Father Oliver had his back to her. He stood by the desk, Katherine's phone to his ear.

"No," the priest said. "Nothing. Katherine's gone. I must say, I'm quite relieved." He paused, listened and then laughed. "I'll see if I can knock some sense into their young heads. You wouldn't believe how resistant some of them are."

Who was the priest talking to?

"Yes, yes," Father Oliver said. "Thank you. We'll speak again."

He hung up the phone. Jem watched him peer around Katherine's office, his gaze resting briefly on the stag head mounted on the wall. He walked around the desk and glanced at the papers spread out on the desktop.

Not so virtuous, eh, Father? What would Katherine do if she knew you were snooping about in her office?

The priest looked up suddenly. Jem moved back.

Had he seen her?

Every muscle tensed as she listened. Then she heard something like a glass being filled. Hesitantly, she moved back to the crack in the door and saw that Father Oliver had helped himself to a glass of something dark. Brandy? She couldn't tell. He fondled the cross at his neck as he sipped the drink.

"Oh, Father," Jem whispered. She slapped a hand to her mouth.

Idiot!

The priest still seemed blissfully unaware of her presence, though. He hummed a hymn to himself as he emptied his glass and set it back on the cabinet by Katherine's desk. He took another last look around and then headed for the office door.

Jem heard the door open and close.

She let out a long breath and slumped against the door. That was too close. If the priest had caught her in Katherine's office, she knew his sermon would have been damning.

Hypocrite.

She turned to scrutinize the small bathroom. Enough light streamed in through the window that she didn't need to turn on the light switch. She glanced at herself in the mirror and noticed it was a cabinet.

"What's in here, then, Katherine?" she said softly to herself as she popped it open.

There were rows of pill bottles. Jem examined the labels.

Aspirin. Lithium.

Lithium. Was Katherine a manic depressive? No big surprise there. Had she strangled her own husband in a fit of rage? Maybe she found him diddling one of her illegal staff members…

Jem spent another five minutes rooting around in the bathroom, even inspecting the waste bin, but found nothing of note.

Nothing except the fact that Katherine hires known criminals. And her husband was strangled to death.

Jem sized up the bathroom window. Probably safer to climb out of there. It opened onto the woods and would give her more cover. She propped it open and heaved herself up onto the ledge.

Damn I'm good.

With a grunt, she dropped down into the woods. Skirting back around the cabins, she realized that even if she hadn't exactly found a smoking gun, Katherine was definitely capable of firing one.

● ● ●

Brady sat on the porch outside the older boys' cabin, shaded from the midday sun. He held a pen in his hand as he considered what to write on his lined sheets of paper. He'd already mailed one letter to Stanley describing the camp and the cabin and who was lame and who was cool. When they kissed each other goodbye, Brady had promised to write to him every day.

Instead, he got high and goofed around with the guys.

It wasn't that he didn't want to write to Stanley, it was just that he couldn't think of anything to say. With most of the campers gearing up for the fun-filled camping trip, he figured that was the best time to seek solace in his boyfriend.

Dear Stanley,

Sorry I haven't written much. They keep us really busy and I don't think they'd like me writing letters to my drop dead gorgeous boy next door.

Brady paused as he thought what he should say next. Starting with an apology and then a compliment was probably the right way to go.

I miss you. And I keep thinking about you getting this letter in the mail. Your eyes light up and then you read it a ton and look at my picture. Do you have any pictures of me? I wish I had one of you so bad. First thing we're doing when I get back is taking Polaroids.

"Hey, behave for Michaela, all right?"

Brady looked up from his letter and found Glen hovering over him, a sporty backpack over his shoulders.

"Yeah, I'll be good. She's chill."

"Good." Glen waved to Lisa, who had the younger girls rounded up nearby. She waved back and he hurried away.

My counselor sucks. He told me I only smoke pot as a way to avoid dealing with my problems. But my biggest problem is I never have enough pot.

A shadow fell over Brady's page and he found Billy standing next to him. "What cha doing?"

"Writing my boyfriend a letter."

"Aw, say hi for me. Just wanted to let you know Michaela wants to see us all outside the mess hall in twenty minutes."

"Sounds good. Thanks."

Billy pulled his long black hair out of his eyes and darted inside the cabin.

My best friend here is a dweeb, but he's all right. He says hi.

I don't know what else to say and my hand's cramping. Guess I should jack off less. (You can help me with that when I get back.)

    Love,

    Brady

He folded the paper into thirds and stuffed it in an envelope with Stanley's address already written on it. He felt homesick just seeing Stanley's name and the address, nearly identical to his own. He hopped off of the porch and looked up at the sun as it hung high in the sky. It would only take him a few minutes to walk through the Camp Genesis archway and make his way along the narrow road to stuff the envelope in the mailbox. He had plenty of time to get back before Michaela started bossing them around.

Once he was out of sight of the cabins, Brady pulled a joint out of his pocket and lit it. He inhaled deeply as he walked along the dirt road to the camp entrance. A slight breeze passed through the trees, picking up his smoke and carrying it down the path.

Brady passed under the camp sign and reached the mailbox. He pulled the lid down and held the envelope up for a moment, not wanting to let go of his connection to Stanley. He gave the envelope a quick kiss and then placed it inside.

He looked at the main road running perpendicular to the dirt road and the shabby CAMP GENESIS sign hanging from a leaning pole. It wouldn't take much to run down the road, toward civilization and a bus ride back home to Stanley.

Brady took a deep drag from the joint and sighed. There was no way he was going to walk a mile or two to town. He turned back where he came from as something slammed into his face.

"What the hell?" Brady stumbled to the ground. The joint fell near his hands. He started to stand, but someone knocked him to the ground. He tried to get a handful of dirt to throw into his assailant's face, but it was too compacted to get enough.

Brady spit out blood as he tried to crawl back up to his feet.

He looked up, and his attacker held a pair of garden shears high above his head.

 "Don't!" Brady screamed as the twin blades drove into his chest. His lungs felt like they were on fire, and he could barely grasp a breath. His attacker left the shears implanted in his body as he grabbed Brady's arms and dragged him off the road and into the woods.

Brady's legs scraped along the ground and twigs and rocks cut him as he was brutally dragged behind the attacker like a ragdoll. Each labored breath stung. As his breath failed him, and the darkness devoured him, his last thoughts were that he should have sent Stanley more letters.

Chapter 16

The camp was eerily empty. Billy thought it resembled a ghost town from an old Western. He imagined a tumbleweed rolling through the deserted camp as the famous whistling music rang in his ears. He sat on his bunk, gazing out the window at the squat cabins that formed Camp Genesis, a feeling of dread nipping at his gut.

He was in trouble. He'd never been in trouble in his life. Other than being shipped off to a gay camp, he'd always been "that guy." The one who sits quietly in class feeling sorry for the teacher when the other students are acting like chimpanzees with ADHD. The one who plays computer games under the bleachers while the cool kids make out above his head.

He'd been caught smoking pot. The look of demonic rage on Katherine's face when she found them still made his stomach flip. He felt sick.

No. Stop being such a dweeb.

Jem wouldn't feel guilty, that was for damn sure. Why was he always so worried about what other people thought? He couldn't even look at Neal without blushing. He'd always been terrified of getting into deep shit, of disappointing his parents. And then he'd disappointed them anyway, simply by being himself. A queer kid.

He knew they were only scared for him. They'd seen the outbreak of AIDS on the frontline of their hospital. What it did to people. The sores. The sickness. They didn't want that for him. But he couldn't help who he was.

Billy kicked a stone off the porch and ambled towards the

main building. He wished Brady hadn't gone off to send that letter. Neal, Kyle and Matthew hadn't returned to the cabin after breakfast, either. Even in the daytime, Cabin Four was creepy without the other guys horsing around, trying to out-gross each other every five minutes. Without them, the cabin seemed sinister, as if there were invisible eyes watching him. A squirrel had scuttled across the roof while he was napping and he'd nearly jumped out of his skin—then hated himself for being such an idiot.

It was two p.m. and all the other campers had already departed, leaving behind the rule-breakers. Billy dreaded to think what chores awaited them.

Will they tell my parents I've been kept back?

A second, new, braver voice answered; the one that had been birthed by Jem and Brady.

Shut up, dweeb.

"Heading my way?" Kyle asked him, appearing on the other side of the path.

"Guess so."

Kyle caught up to him. "Today's going to blow."

"I know."

"But that doesn't blow," Kyle said slowly. He nodded behind Billy.

Billy turned and found Neal jogging toward the cabin, shirtless and sweaty.

"Hey, guys," he called out, raising one hand.

"You put in a workout before they put us to work?" Kyle asked.

"My routine," Neal said with a shrug, slowing down.

"Routines are..." Billy trailed off. Kyle elbowed him. "Great. So great."

"Yeah." Neal hopped up the steps to the porch. "I'm grabbing a quick shower. See you guys in a few."

"Bye." Kyle grabbed Billy's arm and led him away. "Probably best if you're not still staring at the doorway when he comes out."

"Yeah. Thanks. Why are you being nice all of a sudden?"

"It's Misfit Punishment Day. I don't want to waste my energy this early. Besides, I think Neal likes it when I'm, blech, nice."

When they reached the main building, Billy saw Father Oliver was already there with Michaela.

"Prompt as ever, William," the priest beamed. "Thanks for escorting Mr. Majors."

"I'm usually the escort," Kyle drawled, punching Billy patronisingly on the arm. "But yeah, Billy's the best bad kid around."

"I'm not sure that's something to boast about, Mr. Majors," Father Oliver said, although there was a twinkle in his eye.

Billy heard footsteps approaching and turned, expecting to see Jem. Instead, he found Cobb and Steven had joined the group.

"What are you guys doing here?" Kyle asked. Billy couldn't remember Cobb or Steven doing anything to warrant getting banned from the excursion.

They looked sheepish and avoided his eye.

What have they been up to?

"Let's not dwell on the specifics," Father Oliver said. "Now, who's left?" He glanced down at a piece of paper. "Neal, Jem, Matthew and Brady."

"Father Oliver, you gossip," came Jem's unmistakable voice. "My ears were burning all the way from Cabin Two."

"A pleasure as always, Jemima," the priest replied. He was clearly as fond of her as was Billy. Jem winked at Billy. She had her bangles on again, striping her forearms in multicoloured bands. He wondered if she'd raided whichever cupboard was used to store confiscated property.

"Sorry I'm late," Neal said as he strolled up to them. His hair

126

was still wet and Billy felt a blush creep into his cheeks at the sight of him.

"It's fine," Michaela said.

"Ah, Matthew," Father Oliver beamed as he joined the group.

Billy noticed that Neal looked pissed. *He's the kind of guy who would love camping in the wild,* Billy realized. He couldn't help imagining what might have happened if they'd gone on the excursion. Would Neal have crawled into his sleeping bag with him?

Of course not. He's in total denial.

The other, confident voice disagreed. *All he needs is a little encouragement.*

"Billy, that okay with you?"

Billy snapped to and saw that everybody was looking at him, waiting for him to answer Father Oliver. He'd been daydreaming again.

Jem threw an arm around his neck and crushed him to her. "Of course it is," she said. "Bill just can't get enough of me."

What had they just signed up to? Billy realized the priest was handing out their chores.

Brady. Where's Brady?

"Fine," Father Oliver continued. "Kyle and Steven, you can tackle the girls' cabins. Matthew, Neal and Cobb, you'll report to Donny to help out in the kitchen and take care of the mess hall. That just about covers it."

"Who's going to clean up the boys' cabins?" Kyle asked.

"Brady, alone, as his punishment for being late. Michaela and myself will be checking in on all of you periodically, so I needn't remind you that this is not an excuse for slacking off. If you do a good job, then we can have our own campfire with songs and s'mores."

For once, all of the teenagers paid close attention. Even if they weren't interested in religion, there was something about

Father Oliver that was appealing. He was impossible to dislike, and Billy realised everybody wanted to do right by him. Especially if they would be allowed to go camping with the others after they were done.

"Off you go," the priest said. "I'll be checking in with you shortly, as soon as I've located young Brady. I can't imagine he's gone too far."

The small group dispersed.

"Hey Cobb, just because it's called a mess hall doesn't mean you have to mess around with Matthew," Kyle called as he headed off with Steven. "Unless he wants you to, that is."

"Thank you, Kyle," Father Oliver said sternly.

Kyle cracked one of his winning grins, and Jem led Billy through the camp.

"The guy's a grade-A grody," she said. "He should come with a health warning."

"He's all talk. Hey, where do you think Brady is?"

Jem mimed dragging on a joint.

"You think?"

"Come on, have you *met* Brady?" Jem rolled her eyes.

"Where are we going?"

"You really did space out back then." Laughing, Jem elbowed him. "What were you thinking about?"

"Nothing."

"Bet I can guess."

"I don't doubt that. What's our chore?"

"Cleaning out that weird boathouse," Jem said. They rounded a corner at the edge of the camp and Billy spotted a boathouse resting on the shore of the lake. It looked older than the rest of the buildings. The paint was baked hard by the sun and chipping away in chunks. It had been locked for the whole of their stay, but Father Oliver must have unlocked it that morning because the double doors were cracked open.

"Seriously?" Billy said.

"Afraid of a couple of spiders?" Jem teased.

Looking at the boathouse, Billy couldn't help thinking about Tommy and Toombs. What had really happened to them? Neither of them had been seen for days, and the only person who seemed concerned about that was Father Oliver. Now Brady was missing, too.

"Three missing people makes it a pattern," he said quietly.

Jem didn't seem to have heard him. She dragged open the boathouse doors and let out a strangled yell.

A pigeon hurtled out, almost crashing into Jem's face. It missed her by a couple of inches and flapped off into the woods.

"Afraid of a couple of pigeons?" Billy teased.

"Very *not* funny. Come on."

The boathouse made Billy's skin crawl. Nobody had come in here for years, by the look of it. They spent the first hour dragging everything out into the sunshine. Old tools, a tattered umbrella, what looked like the guts of a boat engine. Everything was filthy.

"Why hasn't anybody sorted this place out before now?" Billy wondered out loud.

"Somebody has a serious case of the lazies."

"It reeks in here." Billy pinched his nose.

"Yeah, worse than Donny's cooking."

"You think there's dead rats in here?" he asked.

"Probably. Leave the doors open and let's start airing the place out."

Hot and aching from the physical exertion, Billy kicked off his sandals and wandered over to the lake. The water lapped at the shore and cooled his feet.

"Hey, no slacking." Jem's voice came from inside the boathouse.

"I'm sure they won't mind us taking five minutes."

129

"Have you *met* Katherine?"

"The 'have you met' argument is running out of gas, *compadre*." Billy had never said *"compadre"* before in his life. What was happening to him? He'd had friends before, but nobody like Jem or Brady. They brought out an alien confidence in him. Had it simply been lying dormant?

He snorted. The camp was meant to fix him, but it seemed to be fixing him in a way that nobody intended. His feelings for guys had only intensified, and so had his confidence.

"Hey, Marvin the Martian."

He nearly jumped out of his skin—again.

So maybe the confidence thing only goes so far…

Jem had joined him in the sunshine, her jeans rolled up so she could stroll around in the cool lake water.

"Jeeze, you've got it bad, kid."

"Got what?"

"The love bug. It's all over your cute little face. You know, now's the perfect opportunity to do something about it once and for all. The camp's empty. It'll be easy to get alone with him."

"He…he wouldn't be interested."

"Only one way to find out." She got the glint in her eye that Billy had come to understand signaled impending danger. "We need to make you as alluring as possible. I always find the 'just showered' look goes down best."

"Just showered—" Billy began, but then his mouth was full of water. Jem reached down and scooped up another armful of water and hurled it at him. He stared at her a moment, dripping wet, then he kicked water at her. Shrieking, Jem threw herself at him and they ended up wrestling in the water.

Later, as they dried off in the sun outside the boathouse, Jem lightly punched Billy's arm.

"You going to ask what I found in Katherine's office anytime this millennium?" she asked.

"You actually did it?" Billy asked, glaring at her. Jem had her eyes closed, face tilted toward the sun.

"She didn't even lock the door."

"And?"

"She likes to hire criminals," Jem said, her eyes still shut. "Oh, and her husband was strangled to death and she has a cabinet full of anti-depressants."

"You think she flipped out and made Tommy disappear?"

"I wouldn't put it past her."

"How're the chores going?" a voice asked.

Father Oliver appeared beside them. Billy hadn't even heard him approaching.

"Good." Billy hurried to his feet.

"Yeah, only the odd skeleton," Jem deadpanned. She gave the priest a look that Billy couldn't decipher.

"Glad to hear it," the priest said. "Dinner time in about an hour. Why don't you two finish up here and head on back?"

"Sure," Billy said. "Er, Father. Did you find Brady?"

The priest tensed. His eyebrows knitted together.

"No, William. I didn't."

Once Father Oliver had trotted back into the woods, Billy and Jem returned to their work, neatly putting everything back into the boathouse for a half hour.

As they finished, Jem asked Billy, "So, Don Juan, you going to make your move with Neal, or what?"

Billy sighed. "Life's short, right?"

"That a boy, Bill. Let's lock up here, I want to get back and check the girls' cabins to see if Brady's wandered back yet."

Billy cast Jem a look. A cloud moved over the sun, low in the sky, and he couldn't help shivering.

Chapter 17

Cobb wiped his forehead and his hand came away slick with sweat.

"This bites," he muttered.

He'd gone with Neal and Matthew to the kitchens, where Donny ordered Neal to help him cook and Matthew and Cobb to get cleaning the big dining room. Lucky Neal got everything handed to him on a silver platter because he was so handsome and strong. Cobb would have killed to help Donny make chili in the kitchen instead of laboring, but he kept his mouth shut so the others wouldn't make any fat jokes.

The mess hall wasn't particularly big, but it was big enough to be a pain in the ass to tidy. Matthew wasn't exactly helping, either. He was like a caveman, barely forming anything more than moody grunts as he shoved chairs aside and clumsily jabbed about with a broom.

Cobb wished he'd been teamed up with Jem and Billy. They always had fun. Even at lunch, they had found something to giggle about. Cobb had caught Billy sneaking a glimpse at Neal. It wasn't the first time, and he couldn't blame him. Neal was a catch.

Neal's the type of guy I'll get after I lose this extra weight. Yeah, right.

Instead of hanging out with them, though, giggling over boys, he was stuck with the head case who had attacked Neal. Cobb was concerned for his safety. The morning had passed without incident, but if he said the wrong thing—

"You say something?"

Matthew stared at him from across the hall. Cobb flushed and wondered how quickly he could get to the door.

"Uh," he started. "Just, y'know, this bites is all."

Matthew nodded, eyes dark under his brooding forehead. "Soon as camp lets out, I'm getting my own place," he grunted, sweeping the floor. His muscles rippled under his shirt. Cobb couldn't help noticing. The mix of fear and arousal was surprisingly potent.

"You, er..." He struggled to find something to say. He'd never spoken two words to Matthew or anybody like him before coming to Camp Genesis. Matthew was the kind of guy you glimpsed across the football field, flexing and getting cheered on by skinny girls flashing their pom-poms. Cobb liked going to football games—the hotdogs were good—but he'd never even considered talking to any of the players.

"You think you'll find somewhere?" he hazarded, not daring to look at Matthew. If he looked at him, his tongue would probably stick to the roof of his mouth. Or worse, hang out like a drooling dog's. He busied himself with wiping down the tables.

"Uncle's got a place," Matthew muttered. "S'a dive, but I bet I could afford the rent if I got a job delivering pizzas. They're always hiring and my record's cleaner'n Kyle's asshole."

Cobb's laugh echoed across the mess hall.

Matthew continued sweeping. Cobb noticed the sign above his head that had been hanging there all week.

Smile and the world smiles with you.

This was such a joke. First, they were being punished for being gay. Now they were being punished for not welcoming that punishment. Separated from everybody else. Stuck in camp while the others were roasting marshmallows.

"You ever get sick of talking about being gay?"

Cobb was surprised. Matthew seemed to be trying to have a

133

conversation.

"What do you mean?"

Matthew shrugged. He examined the end of the broom handle, perhaps digging out a splinter. "Dunno. Like, that's not *everything* there is. I couldn't care less if a girl likes another girl, or a guy likes another guy. Who gives a...you know. All they want to talk about round here is sex, as if sex is anything more than a load of rutting and fluids, and isn't over pretty quickly anyway. It's not like we're going through a population crisis or something where everybody *has* to procreate to ensure the survival of mankind. Who gives a fuck who fucks who?"

It was the most Cobb had heard Matthew say all week. His mind reeled. It actually made sense. Just when he'd written him off as a dumb jock who never thought before he acted, he'd revealed a surprisingly sensitive side.

"It's a money-making scam," Cobb said. "People make cash any way they can, and if our parents are stupid enough to hand over money in the hope we'll somehow get fixed, like we're broken robots, then they're the idiots."

Matthew's face darkened.

Crap. Had he said the wrong thing? Fear clenched at him again and Cobb realised the door was actually quite far away. He'd never make it in time if Matthew flipped out.

Then he noticed Matthew was actually staring over his shoulder at something behind him.

"Er," Cobb started.

"Shhh," Matthew hissed. He gripped the broom tighter and moved with slow deliberation like a leopard. Matthew was suddenly beside him. Cobb could smell the sweet tang of his sweat. He mentally shook himself, attempted to slow his hammering heart as Matthew pointed at what he'd been staring at. Cobb looked.

It was the cleaning closet.

What was wrong? Had Matthew seen something?

"What—" he started, but Matthew signaled for him to be quiet. He slowly approached the closet. Cobb watched his back tense, muscles widening and almost doubling in size, then Matthew tore the closet door open.

A mop fell out onto the floor. Matthew bellowed in surprise and kicked it, sending the mop flailing across the mess hall.

"Christ!" Cobb yelled, unable to stop himself. Then he noticed Matthew was doubled over. "Hey, you OK man?" he asked.

Matthew had gone beetroot-red in the face and just when Cobb thought he was going to explode, he finally let out a laugh that boomed through the mess hall. He laughed until it looked painful, clutching at his stomach and panting.

"I thought—" He struggled to speak. "I thought I saw somebody in there."

Cobb didn't know what to say. He found himself laughing, too, infected by Matthew's relentless whooping.

"You sure showed that mop," he said when he couldn't laugh anymore.

"Just call me the Drunken Master," Matthew said, striking a kung-fu pose that made his biceps bulge. "Neeeeee-yah!"

Cobb grew serious again. He couldn't laugh and be friends with somebody that perfect.

"I'm gonna get back to—" he began, then he froze.

A dark shape separated itself from the shadows inside the closet. Before he could yell in surprise, it emerged into the mess hall. Matthew's back was to the closet, so he didn't see his attacker. His face merely warped in confusion as something buried itself in his back and blood pushed through the front of his tight T-shirt.

Cobb wanted to scream. To cry a warning. To communicate his disgust and horror. All he could do was stand and watch. His feet were glued to the floorboards.

"Oh...my..." Matthew was trying to speak. His mouth became a choked red O, a gasping fish out of water. "Oh my...Cobb."

Whatever was in his back was removed, and Matthew's knees gave out beneath him. He crashed to the floor. Cobb felt the reverberations through the floorboards and he still couldn't move.

Matthew didn't move either. Blood gushed from his mouth. Red and angry.

The Closet Man crouched like a giant insect, something metal and wet with blood on his hands.

Matthew's blood.

"Who—" The word left Cobb's mouth in an insubstantial whisper. A vapor. The Closet Man had no face. A black mask covered it and angry, bloodshot eyes blazed out from two cigarette-burn holes at the center. He wore a dark, baggy hoodie, the hood drawn up over his head.

The Closet Man raised a gloved hand and Cobb saw what he was clasping.

Garden shears.

Rusted, mean-looking garden shears. Sticky with... *something.*

The figure rushed at him.

Cobb backed away without thinking, his feet miraculously unstuck from the floor. He couldn't get to the door. The Closet Man stood in the way. Taking a chance, he turned and crashed toward the stage at the back of the mess hall. He couldn't hear his attacker, the Closet Man moved so quietly. Like a spider.

Cobb mounted the stage and flew blindly to the wings, discovering that there was an opening to the backstage area. He rushed through it, finding himself in a long, narrow space. Ropes stretched up into the ceiling and there were panels of light switches. He dodged between the empty paint pots and stools, making for the other side of the stage.

There was a loud creaking sound and he saw that one of the large backdrops propped up against the wall was straining away from the brickwork.

The Closet Man was heaving it away from the wall.

Cobb just had time to throw his hands up when the immense canvas crashed down on top of him.

It felt as if his skull had shattered.

Cobb smashed through the back of the stage and landed on something hard. Floorboards. He was back on the stage. Splintered wood and fabric lay all around him.

He stared up, seeing that the banner above the stage had come unfastened and was swinging above his head.

The Closet Man towered over him.

"Please," Cobb wheezed, unable to catch his breath. The dark shadow raised the garden shears.

They were plastered with Matthew's blood.

The blades plunged for his chest.

The last thing Cobb saw was the stage banner fluttering down to blanket him.

Smile and the world smiles with you.

Chapter 18

"I'm too pretty to do manual labor," Kyle whined.

"I'm cute, and I'm still doing work," Steven said.

"We can discuss who's hot and who's not after you finish cleaning up." Kyle tossed his broom to the floor in a huff. He and Steven had cleaning duty in the younger girls' cabin, and Kyle couldn't stand it anymore. His muscles ached, and he was starting to get hungry. Michaela had checked in on them twice and even helped clean her cabin, but Kyle couldn't help but imagine the others were having a much better time. When Kyle complained that the others got to cook instead of clean, Michaela told him Matthew and Cobb were working just as hard as they were in the mess hall.

"Get back to work," Steven said. "The sooner we finish, the sooner we get s'mores."

"Pronounce the letter S, just once," Kyle said, hands on his hips.

"I'm sorry my lisp offends you. There's plenty offensive about you." Steven shook his head and kept cleaning.

"Like what?"

"Nothing."

"No, this is the most I've heard you say all week. Out with it."

"Fine, Princess High Horse." Steven threw his cleaning supplies on the floor and spun toward Kyle. "My biggest problem can be fixed with speech therapy. You can't fix being a classless slut."

Kyle gasped. "I have class." Steven gave him an *oh really* look. "What? I do. Don't I?"

"You strut around naked, you're mean, and you don't even want to better yourself. The whole ex-gay thing is lame, but there's other stuff you could get out of being at camp. You could learn about nature and find some exercise you like and make friends. Instead, you're too concerned about seducing a troubled jock, which would probably be really bad for his state of mind. But you don't care about that, either. And on top of it all, you're an asshole to the others. Do you have to call Cobb fat and Matthew short every single day? I would feel sorry for you because you must be really lonely, but then I remember you bring it on yourself."

Kyle turned around to make sure Steven wouldn't see his tears. "I'm going to take a break."

As Kyle left, he heard Steven say, "I'm not dealing with all this drama BS any more. I'm going to put my Walkman on, crank up my tunes, and mind my own business while I clean."

Kyle stepped out of the cabin and into the warm air outside. He sniffled and sat down on the edge of the steps. Another wasted summer. He couldn't make any real friends, and he'd return home to his parents a complete failure, just like the year before.

I should go back in and help Steven. I could tell Mom and Dad I made one friend. A nerdy black kid. See, I'm a winner.

Kyle stood back up and reached for the door handle.

Just open the door and apologize.

He couldn't do it. Steven's words were too fresh. The worst part was that Steven had been absolutely right. And Kyle had been an asshole every day, especially to Cobb and Matthew. He couldn't apologize to Steven just yet, but the other two were a different story. They'd never said anything that mean about him. At least not to his face.

Kyle hopped down the front steps and made his way across the camp to find the others. With most everyone out in the woods enjoying s'mores, the campground felt deserted. It wasn't supposed to be so isolated until after lights out.

Kyle pictured everyone camping and having a good time. They weren't working. They were even supposed to take the night off from their gender-based activities. The girls were probably cutting wood and the boys were cooking. Just the way it was supposed to be.

As Kyle walked through the slowly darkening camp, he felt eyes on his back. In school, he'd loved that feeling, but out there, it had a different feeling altogether. Kyle spun around, the hair on the back of his neck rising, but there was no one there. He chided himself for acting so foolishly.

No one's out to get me. Everything's fine. Relax.

Kyle shivered as the wind picked up. He turned his back into it, his yellow hair fluttering over his eyes. He reached the mess hall and knocked on the door, butterflies in his stomach.

Don't be a nervous bitch. Fatty and Shorty, um, Cobb and Matthew, will accept your apology. Be cool.

He knocked again, but no one answered. Had they already finished in the mess hall? He opened the door, allowing some light in. Squinting, Kyle couldn't tell if it had been cleaned or not.

"Anybody home? Shor—Matthew? Cobb?" The door creaked open, swallowed into the shadows. "If you guys are that fast, Steven could use some help. Guys?"

He strolled into the mess hall.

"If I find you guys wrestling under the tables, I want you to know I have two rules about that," he called. "First, nothing above the face except when I ask for it. Second, nobody finishes until I—"

He stopped.

Something was wrong with the stage at the back of the room. It didn't look right. Perhaps it was the dim light playing tricks on him, but the back wall seemed to have collapsed onto the stage. He strode toward it, slipped and hit the floor with a cry.

"My ass—" he started, then sucked in a breath. His hands were wet. He raised them and every hair on his arms prickled.

Red.

Thick red liquid was smeared all over his hands. Then he saw Matthew. He lay facedown in a dark pool. His eyes were wide open in a frozen expression of horror.

"Matthew," Kyle began. He couldn't stop looking at him. How still and pale he was. How red the red looked in comparison to his bleached, dead face.

Dead face.

"Blood," Kyle gasped. Finally, he managed to look away. He stared fearfully up at the stage. Now that his eyes had adjusted to the dim light, he saw the figure lying still amid the debris. The curly hair. The unmistakably stocky build.

"Fatty," Kyle whispered. His mind started racing.

Oh God, oh God, oh God, oh God.

His vision blurred, he wanted to scream, but he couldn't move. He couldn't look away from Cobb's prone body until he noticed something even stranger. Kyle slowly managed to get to his feet. Fearfully, he approached the stage.

Cobb lay in a pool of blood. One of his hands was covered in it, and by his side, he had scrawled something messily on the floor.

CLOSET MAN.

What does that mean?

Peering at all that blood, the panic rose in Kyle's chest. He needed help, he needed to escape, he needed to warn the others.

The others!

He bolted out of the mess hall. Where was the killer? Who

was the killer? Who else was dead? What did "Closet Man" mean? Was that who had killed Cobb and Matthew?

A twig snapped several feet away. Kyle stopped in his tracks and threw his body against a tree. He held his hands away from his body. Hands that were sticky with blood.

Someone was walking along the path nearby. Quietly.

Michaela, Father Oliver, or the killer?

Kyle took a step around the tree to peek out, and he snapped a twig. *Damn it.* The shadow of a person rippled across a tree, but Kyle couldn't see who it was. Did he, or she, know Kyle was there? He felt like they'd entered a tense stand-off, neither knowing who was there. Normally, he would have called out, or made some joke, but not now. The Closet Man could be anywhere.

He bent low to the ground, crouching in the shadows, and carefully made his way behind a nearby tree. He spotted the other figure sneaking around further down the path.

Katherine!

He stood up, prepared to run back to get Steven for help, but Katherine spun around.

"Kyle Majors!"

"Katherine Creevey!" They stared each other down. "What are you doing?"

"I could ask you the same thing."

"Father Oliver sent me back here to check on things. He told me Brady's disappeared, too. He's out looking for the boy, and I find you sneaking around the camp instead of finishing your chores. Explain yourself."

"Matthew and Cobb are dead."

"That's not remotely funny."

"No, it isn't."

She looked down, seemed to notice his red hands.

Neither moved. Twelve feet separated them. If he ran, could

she catch up with him? Did she have a knife on her?

"Come here," Katherine said quietly.

"No."

"Kyle."

"What?"

Thud!

Katherine's eyes rolled up into the back of her head and she crumpled to the ground.

Kyle jumped back, and then spotted Jem standing over Katherine, holding a large branch in both hands.

Jem looked from Katherine up to Kyle. "Time to get some answers out of this bitch."

Chapter 19

Jem tossed the branch to the ground and ignored her shaking hands.

No going back now.

"You knocked her out!" Kyle yelled. Jem looked at him. His infuriating grin was nowhere to be seen. He was deathly pale, his eyes big and round—and there was red on his T-shirt where he'd wiped his hands.

"What happened to you?" she asked, then shook her head. "We haven't got time. Help me drag her to the office before she comes to."

"Drag her? Are you nuts?"

"Kyle, just help me."

"You probably killed her, or at least gave her brain damage."

Jem ignored him. She'd just do it herself. It wasn't that far to Katherine's office and Katherine was bony as hell; she couldn't be that heavy. Jem grabbed the camp owner's wrists and began hauling her across the dirt.

"Christ," Kyle muttered, and together they hoisted her off the ground.

"There's red on you," Jem said as they headed for the office. "Did you find Matthew and Cobb?"

Kyle shot her a suspicious look. "How did you know?"

"Billy went back to his cabin and I thought there might be snacks in the mess hall…"

Kyle still looked wary.

"It wasn't me, I swear," Jem snapped. "If I was going to kill somebody, I wouldn't hack them to pieces like that. Too suspicious."

"Did you see what Cobb wrote?" Kyle asked.

"Closet Man. What do you think that means?"

"No fucking idea."

They clambered up the steps and Jem shoved the office door open with her foot. The stuffy air inside rushed out at them.

Good, it'll make it even more uncomfortable for Katherine.

They set the camp owner down on the chair behind the desk. In her smart suit she looked like a lifeless mannequin. Her chin rested on her chest.

Jem started rummaging through the desk. She grabbed the duct tape in the top drawer and wrapped several layers around Katherine's wrists and arms of the chair.

She stepped away, satisfied.

Not bad for my first time tying somebody up.

She turned to look for Kyle.

He'd retreated to the far corner and leaned against the wall, staring at his palms without blinking.

"It's just shock, it'll wear off," Jem said.

"They're both dead," Kyle choked. "Who the hell did it?"

Jem looked at Katherine.

"Suspect number one," she muttered. There was a cooler in the corner filled with water bottles. She grabbed one, tossed it to Kyle and took another. Unscrewing the top, she dumped the whole lot over Katherine's head.

"Wakey wakey."

Katherine spluttered and jerked awake in the chair. Her wet hair clung to the sides of her face and her eyes bulged wide. The surprise quickly turned to anger.

"What do you think you're doing?" she demanded, struggling against the duct tape. "Untie me at once!"

"Quiet," Jem said.

"You might want to listen to her, Katherine," Kyle murmured, lowering the water bottle, his lips wet. "I've never seen her this nuts before."

Jem put her hands on her hips and tried to look intimidating. She'd never read Nancy Drew, but she knew she was a detective. Jem imagined herself as a purple-haired version of her, only way cooler. Maybe with a motorbike and a closet full of sharp implements and a cute blonde secretary.

"You two are in big trouble," Katherine snapped, though her voice was weaker than Jem had ever heard it. Her head must be really hurting. "You're both expelled."

"Consider us ex-campers by choice," Jem shot back. "This place is turning into a bloodbath and you know why."

"Bloodbath?"

"Matthew and Cobb are dead," Jem said.

"Skip ahead," Kyle said. "I already told her that."

"Well they are. And Brady never showed this morning. And Tommy and Toombs have been gone for days. They're all dead, aren't they?"

Be strong. Be tough. Break this bitch.

Katherine didn't answer. She looked at the floorboards.

"AREN'T THEY?!" Jem yelled, grabbing Katherine's hair and yanking her face up.

"I don't know!" Katherine yelled back. "Maybe. Probably."

Jem let go, surprised at her own ferocity. Perhaps the hair-pulling was going too far.

No. She deserves it. She's responsible.

"Start talking," she told Katherine.

"She's not going to talk..." Kyle began behind her.

Jem grabbed a pair of scissors from the desk. "If she values that Toni & Guy haircut she will."

Katherine shot her a look filled with such venom that Jem nearly feared for her own life. She faltered, thought about

146

checking the duct tape in case Katherine had managed to wriggle her skinny wrists free. Then Katherine's body relaxed, the fight leaving her eyes as she gazed toward the floor.

"The troubles started our second year," she said quietly, the Southern drawl more apparent than ever. "I set up the Genesis program with my husband, Brian. He inherited a lovely farmhouse from his grandfather. The first summer was such a success that we had parents from all across the country contacting us. We decided to hold two summer sessions the next year to fit them all in. But then, at the end of the first session, there was a fire."

"Yeah," Jem said. "Michaela told us about that. Did anyone die?"

"Not then."

"So you guys moved shop?" Kyle asked.

"Yes. Brian and I turned the Genesis program into Camp Genesis. The first session started out so well. Then Brian, my husband... We found him hanged in this office. Suicide. Or at least it looked like it." Her voice cracked with grief.

Jem stood firm, scissors still clasped in her hands.

Let her talk. Don't take pity on her.

"We kept the camp open, we kept the suicide quiet," Katherine continued. "We told the kids Brian had gone away. Nobody suspected a thing. But then one night..." She squeezed her eyes shut. "Miles..."

"Who's Miles?" Jem asked.

"He was a camper here. He ran off into the woods with another boy. They... Well, we found them the next morning. They were both dead." She choked back a sob. "My Miles..."

"Your Miles?" Jem asked.

"He was my son," Katherine said, tears coming. "My beautiful son. And now he's dead."

"You enrolled your own son at an anti-gay camp?" Kyle said.

"That's sick."

"It's the reason Brian and I started the Genesis program," Katherine cried. "He was sick! He needed help!"

"Somebody definitely helped him," Jem said sharply. "Let me guess, they never found the killer?"

Katherine shook her head. Her eyes glazed over. She seemed to be reliving the events of three years ago. "The police questioned everybody. The staff. The other campers. Locals. Nobody was arrested. There was no evidence. Nothing." She trembled. "Nothing. Eventually, the police ruled it a murder suicide to appease the parents and reporters."

"So of course you decided to reopen the camp," Kyle said, joining Jem.

"It was a tragedy," Katherine said, her voice quiet and fragile. "We couldn't let that stop our work. I took a year off for the news outlets to grow tired of the story, and reopened last summer with one, smaller session."

"I remember," Kyle said. "There were only twenty of us."

"And it went well," Katherine said. "Once the parents saw the camp was safe, I was inundated with requests. One boy had waited four years to come here."

"Yeah, this place is so great that you got college kids and ex-cons to work here," Kyle said.

"That's not true," Katherine said.

"Liar!" Jem shouted. "I saw their job applications."

"Only the cooks, and nothing dangerous. Just drugs and arson," Katherine explained. "To help rehabilitate them. And money's tight. I'll do whatever it takes to turn Camp Genesis into the success it deserves to be. I vowed to run this camp in Miles' honor until the day I die."

"You're even sicker than I gave you credit for," Kyle said. "You really think your son would be happy about you running a place like this? In his honor? He was gay!"

"He was troubled."

"He's dead, and he wouldn't be if it wasn't for you," Kyle continued accusingly. "You killed him! And you killed everybody else in the camp!"

"No!"

"You're punishing us all, aren't you?" Jem demanded. "You can't accept that you were responsible for Miles, so you're blaming everybody else. Innocent kids. You killed Tommy and Brady and Matthew."

"And Cobb," Kyle added.

Katherine shook her head. "I didn't kill anybody," she pleaded. "I could never..."

She fell silent.

Kyle pulled Jem away from Katherine.

"You buy it?" he asked.

Jem didn't know what to think. Katherine seemed unhinged, but was she a murderer? All she could see in the camp owner's face was grief. Maybe a bit of mania. Manic grief, perhaps.

"I don't know," she said.

"I say we go look for Father Oliver and the others," Kyle said. "If the killer's still out there, this Closet Man, they're all in danger."

"And if Katherine's the killer?"

"We leave her tied up in here," Kyle reasoned. "Win, win."

"Nobody's winning in this place."

Jem looked at Katherine. She couldn't help feeling sorry for her. The camp owner's head was lowered to her chest again. She whispered prayers, her wet and tangled hair falling into her lap. She looked like a broken doll.

"She's not going anywhere," Jem said. "Come on, let's go find the others."

Chapter 20

Billy reached the nearly-deserted camp quicker than he would have liked. He used his time on the walk to imagine what he would say to Neal.

Hey, I know you don't like talking about stuff, but if you ever do, I'd love to listen.

Hi, Neal, I love you.

Neal, my man, want to make out?

I'm a guy. You're a guy. Let's just do this thing already.

He would probably end up stuttering and just run away, and Jem would never let him hear the end of it. He heard rock music blaring from the kitchen as he approached and wondered if Donny would even let him talk to Neal.

Billy stood outside the screen door and peered inside. His mouth watered when he smelled cooking meat, but he didn't see anyone tending to the steaming pots.

"Hey, anyone home? Matthew, Cobb?" Hopefully, one of the other guys could distract him long enough to figure out what to say.

Neal stepped in front of the door, making Billy's pulse speed up. "Hey, Billy, what's up? You and Jem all done out there?"

"Uh, uh, yes. Matthew and Cobb in the kitchen? Are they in the kitchen, I mean. I can speak."

"Nope. Donny told them to clean up the mess hall. I started helping him with the chili for tonight, and then he took off a while ago." Neal shrugged. "So what are you up to?"

"Walking. Just wanted to say hi. I'm pretty grody from

cleaning, I should change clothes before dinner." *Don't wuss out. Let him know you're interested!* "You should, um, change before dinner, too."

"Yeah, I smell like sauce," Neal said. "Go on, I'm going to clean up and I'll see you there."

"Cool."

Neal turned back to the kitchen and Billy ran as hard as he could back to Cabin Four.

I did it, I did it. Wait, what did I do exactly? Right, told him he smells. Smooth.

After changing his T-shirt and shorts, Billy perched on the edge of Neal's bed. There were a few battered Polaroids tacked to the wall beside it. A younger Neal in his football jersey, grinning as if he didn't have a care in the world. There was a woman, too, holding a baby. His mom, maybe. The baby was cute enough to be Neal.

"Hey man."

Billy looked up as Neal came into the cabin.

"I'm beat," the jock sighed, dragging his T-shirt up and over his head. He dumped it on the floor. "Cleaners get a bad rep, but that is one tiring gig."

Billy smiled nervously. What did Neal have to go and take his T-shirt off for? Now there was no way he could look at him.

"Sorry," he said, realizing he was still sitting on Neal's bed. His own bunk was on top. He got up quickly, but hesitated when Neal perched on Kyle's bed instead, just opposite him.

"No worries, it's not like it's really mine," Neal said. "My real bed's far more comfortable."

Is Neal flirting?

Don't be a dummy. He's only making conversation.

A dusky light filtered into the cabin. The sun was on its way down. They were alone in Cabin Four with the evening air. It was almost romantic, despite the shabbiness of the dwelling.

"You have fun today?" Neal asked. He stretched and Billy couldn't resist looking at him, admiring every muscle as it tightened under the skin.

"If you call cleaning out an old boathouse fun," he murmured, aware that he was staring and that was probably considered creepy. He ruffled his hair and dust came out of it.

"Time to hit the showers, huh?" Neal grinned.

He's flirting!

Billy's heart hammered. It couldn't be. Why now? Had Neal been waiting just like he had? Waiting until they were alone, away from the other guys and their relentless banter?

"Yeah, I guess," he stammered awkwardly.

"This place is kinda nice without the guys," Neal commented, looking around. "Kyle's so loud. He reminds me of guys back home."

"There are gay guys where you're from?"

"Not many, they sort of clump together in packs. I see them some weekends, squawking like parrots in the park. They get drunk there and sing rock songs."

"Kyle's not like anybody I ever met," Billy said.

"What's that thing they say? 'Out and proud.' That's Kyle. He couldn't be more out if his hair was dyed rainbow."

Does Neal like Kyle after all? It almost sounded like Neal admired him. Disappointment fell on Billy like a dead weight and his shoulders slumped.

"You do that a lot."

Billy looked at Neal. "Do what?" he asked.

"Go into your head. Half the time I can't tell what you're thinking. The other half you're looking at me."

Billy blushed. "I—I—" he yammered. He felt like he was floating up into the ceiling. He couldn't feel the mattress under him anymore. Neal's mattress.

"It's cool." Neal flashed him that heart-melting grin and Billy blushed even more. "Kyle does it, too. I don't mind. Well, maybe Kyle. I'd never... But you..."

It was Neal's turn to look nervous. Weirdly, it made Billy feel more confident.

"Look, I, uh—"

Billy started picking at his nails, something he never did.

"You alright?" Neal asked.

"I, uh," Billy started. "I guess there's... There's something I was hoping to talk to you about."

You sound like you're in a business meeting. Chill out!

"Should I be nervous?" Neal asked and Billy locked eyes with him.

"I've never done this," he started. "I guess..." He looked from his pasty, skinny legs to Neal. Perfect, tanned, buff Neal. His resolve shriveled into nothing. "I can't," he said, standing up. He wasn't brave. The newfound confidence wasn't real. He couldn't tell Neal how he really felt. He imagined Neal laughing. Doubling over and laughing until there were tears. Then he'd tell everybody that poor little Billy had a crush, and they'd all laugh, too.

Neal stood up and said, "Hey, man, whatever it is, you can tell me."

His torso was smooth in the gauzy evening light. Like those perfect models from magazines and TV. Billy tried to ignore it, like he wasn't there.

"I should shower," he mumbled miserably. Neal moved closer. Billy backed up and felt the mattress against his calves. There was nowhere else to go.

"Billy, you're so sweet," Neal said. "You're shaking."

He raised a big hand and squeezed Billy's arm.

He was so close Billy could feel his breath against his cheek.

"Tell me," Neal urged softly.

"I..."

Billy couldn't think clearly. He was imagining it. He was dreaming. How was it possible that Neal was this close to him? Gorgeous Neal who everybody had the hots for.

"Tell me," Neal whispered again, and this time his lips brushed Billy's. He felt Neal's eyelashes flutter against his own.

"I…I like you," Billy murmured and it felt amazing to say it. A sweet relief. His entire body was on fire. He was hard as a rock. Pumping with blood and energy. The heat from Neal's body was volcanic.

"I know," Neal said.

Billy felt a sharp, tearing pain. Both ice cold and white hot in his abdomen. He tried to pull away, but Neal grabbed the back of his head with his hand.

"Tell me again," Neal whispered.

The pain was unbearable. A spearing torment, as if something were buried in his gut.

Is this love?

"I…I love you," Billy breathed, trying to forget the pain. The agony and the ecstasy of Neal's grip. He peered down and didn't know what he was seeing. It didn't make sense.

Something was buried in his stomach. It looked like a knife— and Neal's hand was clenched around the handle.

"Kiss me," Neal sighed. "Kiss me."

"I—" Billy struggled. "What have you done?"

"Kiss me."

Billy attempted to pull away from him. "Please," he whispered, but Neal's grip on the back of his head was like iron.

"Kiss me," Neal begged. Tears stained his cheeks and a throbbing, irresistible heat came off him. *"Kiss me."*

Billy pushed his lips to Neal's. Firm, dry, perfect.

He cried out as the blade was removed. Coldness flooded through him and he didn't know where he was. Neal shoved him back onto the bed.

"You want me," Neal hissed. His face was gaunt, stretched into a bony grimace.

Billy's vision swam. He was dimly aware of Neal climbing on top of him, heavy and solid. Solid muscle. Blood smeared across his bare chest.

"You want me," Neal repeated, and the knife in his hand was covered in blood, too. Billy peered down again and saw that he was covered in dazzling red. Soaked through. He was so cold. His whole body tingled. Shivered. Tried to make sense of what was happening.

"Goodbye," Neal said.

The blade came down again, flashing repeatedly as it caught the dying sunlight, and all Billy could think as his body opened and bled was, "I loved you."

Chapter 21

Michaela set her well-worn copy of *The Clan of the Cave Bear* down. She couldn't concentrate on the prehistoric tribe as it only reminded her of her misbehaving charges. Something nagged at the back of her mind that she couldn't quite place. She should have felt at ease. She should have been confident and in command, but instead she felt jittery.

Maybe it was how quiet the camp had been since most everyone left on the camping trip. Michaela couldn't wait for the kids to finish their chores so they could have their Island of Misfit Toys fun. Father Oliver would play the guitar, she'd sing, and the kids would clap along. They'd eat and everyone would feel much better.

And I won't have any more of those thoughts.

She glanced at her wristwatch. Better to keep busy. Better check on the boys and Jcm again and talk and make plans than to be left alone to think. She decided to check on Steven and Kyle, her problem angel, first.

Fighting her sadness, Michaela left the cabin and made her way to the younger girls' bunk. She opened the door and found Steven sweeping with a broom, sashaying to whatever music played on his headphones. Katherine would have had a fit and made him sweep like a real man, but Michaela couldn't bring herself to chastise him.

"Steven. Steven!"

He jumped and spun around, one hand on his chest. "Oh, you startled me. What's going on?"

"Just wanted to check in with you boys since it's almost dinner time. How are you making out? And where's Kyle?"

"He's not here."

Michaela sighed. "What happened?"

Steven planted his hands on his slender hips, telling her, "He thinks he's too pretty to work, so I told him he's a jackass. Then he looked like he was going to cry and he left. I'd feel bad about it, but someone needed to put him in his place. I mean, he is so pretty, but, um, sorry. I mean, I don't know what I'm supposed to say. I just want to get my work done."

"Okay, okay. We can talk about the pretty comment later. I'll find Kyle and talk to him. Thanks for being honest, Steven."

"No problem." He put his headphones back on and returned to his work.

Michaela stepped out of the cabin and wondered where to go after Kyle. The last thing she needed was someone disappearing on her watch. If the boy was upset, he'd either want to be alone, or seek comfort with one of the other guys.

He must be flirting with Neal in the kitchen. At least Donny's there to make sure nothing gets out of hand.

Michaela left the porch and headed toward the kitchen. Even if Kyle wasn't there, she needed to check on Neal, and she wouldn't mind a quick snack. There were usually granola bars available, and she had the feeling she'd need a pick-me-up before the night was over.

But after she checked her wristwatch, Michaela realized it was nearly dinner time anyway. Best to make the rounds and send everyone to the mess hall. She turned around and jogged over to the older boys' cabin.

She reached the cabin and heard soft whispers from inside.

If I catch Kyle in bed with someone, so help me...

She opened the door as quietly as possible, so she could catch whoever it was in the act. As the door opened, the light from outside poured into the dim cabin. One of the boys, shirtless, knelt over another in the bottom bunk.

"Boys, stop what you're doing this instant!" She sounded more like Katherine than she ever wanted.

The shirtless camper turned around.

Neal!

She never would have suspected Neal of fooling around with anybody; he'd half convinced her he really was at camp due to a misunderstanding. And it wasn't Kyle he was with, but Billy.

Michaela paused. Was that blood on Neal's chest?

Neal took a step toward her, his voice shaking. "He tried to seduce me."

"What's happened? Billy, are you—" Billy's head rolled to the side, blood pouring out of his mouth and nose. His eyes were wide and lifeless. "Oh my God!"

Shock froze her to the spot. What the hell was going on here? Neal had been on top of Billy, and now Billy looked...

Neal licked his lips and took another step toward Michaela. "He had to be punished. Isn't that why we're here? Punish our wicked ways. You're supposed to keep us on the straight and narrow. But you haven't."

"Put the knife down." She backed up hesitantly, trying to keep the distance.

"You're a failure, just like the others."

The jock sprinted toward her. With a yell, Michaela dove out of his path, crashing through the cabin door and down the steps to the ground. This was madness. Neal seemed to have lost his mind. He was unhinged—and he was still coming at her.

She needed help. She needed to warn the others. Her chest tightening with panic, Michaela raced toward the center of the camp, but Neal was right behind her.

She tried not to look behind her, but he was even closer when she glanced back. The veins bulged in his neck. Before she knew it, he tackled to her the dirt.

Michaela threw a blind punch but it didn't seem to do any good.

"Why are you doing this?" she asked as he raised his knife.

"You're all a bunch of alcoholics, druggies, failures, and deviants."

His lips peeled back over his teeth, sweat sliding down the side of his face.

She tried to scurry away from him, but Neal plunged the knife into her side. Michaela screamed, but he was the only one who heard her.

He stabbed her a second time. A brilliant shock of pain shot through her.

Michaela summoned the last of her strength and slammed her fist into his face. He fell back long enough for her to scramble to her knees, but the damage was already done. She felt faint and heard him chuckle as she collapsed back to the ground.

Chapter 22

Kyle didn't know what to do. How could the entire world go so crazy in such a short amount of time? Yesterday, he'd been worried about whether or not he could hook up with the hottest guy at camp, and today he had to fight for his life.

Camp was so much better last year.

"Where should we look for the others first?" he asked Jem. "We probably shouldn't split up."

"I don't know. Your cabin, I guess."

"You need to untie me this instant," Katherine said. "We'll call the police. The entire department will be here within minutes, and we'll make sure everyone else is all right."

"Not everyone *is* all right," Jem said.

The faces of Creepy Toombs, Brady, Tommy, Matthew, and Cobb flashed through Kyle's mind. He had a bad feeling there were more bodies out there.

"No," Katherine said. "I will not allow this horror to continue. Listen to me, you need to untie me, and we'll get the police."

"We don't need you to call the police," Kyle said. He made a show of grabbing the heavy phone receiver and raising it to his ear.

He started to spin the rotary to 911, but he didn't hear any dial tone.

"What's wrong?" Jem asked.

Kyle set the receiver down and tried it again, but it still didn't work.

"Yeah, it's dead."

Damn! Shit! Fuck!

"Okay, it's not Katherine, right?" Kyle asked Jem. He was starting to think three of them together were better than two.

"I don't know!"

"It's not me!"

Knock knock knock!

The three of them jumped, spinning toward the front door.

"Who is it?" Kyle whispered to Jem.

"I don't know!"

"Check it," he hissed at her.

"You check it."

Knock knock knock!

"Untie me and *I'll* open it," Katherine said.

"Should we?" Kyle asked Jem.

"I don't know."

Knock knock knock!

Kyle took a breath and then approached the office door. Screwing up his courage, he drew it open.

Michaela lay on the steps leading up to the office. She clutched her side, which oozed blood. She was unbelievably pale, her lips almost purple.

Katherine screamed out and jerked in the chair, straining against the duct tape.

Michaela looked at Kyle, her hazel eyes registering pain. "Neal..." she whispered, blood coming from her mouth and trickling down her chin. Speaking seemed to hurt. Everything looked like an effort. "It's Neal."

"Get out of the way!" Jem cried, shoving Kyle aside to get to Michaela.

But it was too late. Before Jem could reach her, Michaela's head dropped to the porch floor. She lay perfectly still. Icy shivers ran down Kyle's spine. He thought he was going to throw up.

"Is she—?" he asked.

"Shut the goddamned door!" Katherine shouted.

Kyle slammed it shut, closing off their view of Michaela's body, and locked it.

"Neal?" Kyle asked them. That didn't make any sense. He was intense, sure, but no killer. Or was he? He had the strength to hunt the others down, and the moments of severity. "Neal's the Closet Man?"

"Of course it's one of you cursed children," Katherine spat. "Untie me."

"Do it," Kyle said.

Nodding, Jem ripped off the duct tape around Katherine's wrists. The older woman flexed her arms and jumped to her feet.

"Barricade the door," she ordered.

"Shouldn't we make sure Billy's okay first?" Jem asked.

"Don't be stupid. Block the door. Now."

"With what?" Jem asked.

"Anything."

Kyle helped Jem pull a bookshelf across the wall, covering the door frame.

"What else?" Jem asked.

"We need weapons," Katherine said. She grabbed the scissors from her desk.

"What about those antlers on the dead animals?" Kyle asked, gesturing toward the grotesque hunting trophies on the wall.

"They look sharp enough," Jem said. "But I don't know about snapping them off and getting all stabby with them."

"Do something," Katherine said.

"What?" Jem asked.

Kyle dropped his head in his hands. So many of them were dead. And now Michaela? And Neal was to blame? Neal!

"Why would Neal do this?" he asked.

"Maybe he couldn't handle coming to this freakshow of a camp," Jem spat.

Katherine looked ashen. Kyle asked her, "You know anything about that?"

"Neal was signed up to come to camp four years ago for the second summer session," Katherine said, her voice hollow.

"But you had the fire first," Jem stated.

"Yes. And then he was rescheduled to take part in the second session the following year."

Kyle couldn't help marvelling at her memory. Katherine knew her stuff, no matter how crazy she was.

"But first your husband and son were...you know...murdered," he said.

"We reopened last year with a smaller group," Katherine said. "His parents wanted him to attend, but I had to make cuts."

"Which is the only reason he didn't massacre everyone last summer," Kyle concluded. A near miss for him, then. If Neal had attended camp last year, who knew what he might have done. Kyle resisted pointing the finger at Katherine. She was to blame for Neal's psychotic behavior, he was sure of it.

If Neal had been left without counseling and never attended camp, who was to say he wouldn't have sliced and diced the first woman who tried to get into his pants?

Was a psycho a psycho no matter what? Had Camp Genesis simply brought it out in him? Kyle struggled to find an answer and, realizing that it really didn't matter if Neal was on the rampage, he gave up.

"I've done everything in my power to help you!" Katherine announced, her nostrils flaring. "I've sacrificed everything, and I will not let this maniac destroy my legacy!"

Katherine slashed at the air with her scissors, pressing the twin blades together in quick *swish swish* sounds. Kyle thought she had never looked so deranged.

Something thudded in the adjacent room. Kyle and Jem shared a look.

"What's in the other room?" he asked.

"It's just a bathroom," Jem said.

"The window..." Katherine began.

Kyle and Jem started pushing the bookcase away from the front door as the bathroom door creaked open. Neal stood in the shadows of the bathroom, his bare chest heaving in and out, a bloody knife sticking out of his pocket. Kyle couldn't believe the image in front of them. Neal looked totally different.

This is really happening. He's going to kill us all.

"You murdered my Miles!" Katherine shrieked suddenly, swiping the scissors at Neal.

Neal ducked out of Katherine's way with the grace of a dancer and grabbed her by the throat.

"And it still didn't stop you from running this fucking camp!" he spat. "You should've gotten the hint after I torched your farmhouse and killed your husband."

Katherine squirmed like an eel in his grasp, her face contorting with a disturbing combination of mania and grief. She struggled against him as he picked her up off the floor and charged at the wall, slamming her against the stuffed deer trophy.

Kyle watched as the antlers pierced through Katherine's body, blood pouring out from where they speared her.

As Katherine gurgled, Neal pulled free from her grip, leaving her suspended by the antlers.

Nearly overcome, Kyle and Jem managed to move the bookcase far enough to open the door. Kyle was damned if he was going to end up the same way as Katherine. She didn't even look dead, suspended and twitching, blood oozing down her legs...

"Where do you think you're going?" Neal demanded.

"Fuck you!" Jem screamed.

"Maybe we could try out some of Katherine's corrective therapy," Neal said with a wicked grin.

He started after Jem and Kyle, but Katherine jerked unexpectedly as she hung against the wall, using what looked like her dying breath to bury the scissors in Neal's back.

Neal grunted and stopped in his tracks.

"Go, *go*," Kyle urged, pushing Jem out the door.

Unleashing a roar, Neal dragged the scissors out and buried them deep in Katherine's chest. A final, exhausted breath escaped her lungs and then she was still.

Refusing to bear witness to any more carnage, Kyle dashed out of the cabin after Jem, whose sneakers flashed white in the dark as she raced ahead of him.

"Hurry!" Jem shouted back.

His fists clenched, Kyle ran as hard as he could. His chest burned and his knees ached, but he couldn't slow down. He couldn't let Neal catch them. He followed Jem as she weaved around the cabins. He didn't know if she had a plan or was running entirely on instinct.

Neal bellowed behind them. It was a tormented sound that echoed through the camp.

Jem dove toward Cabin Four with Kyle right behind her. They kept the lights off.

"Billy?" Jem whispered.

Someone moaned from one of the beds. Kyle jumped and watched Jem approach. As his eyes adjusted to the darkness, he recognized the nerdy camper curled up on Neal's bunk.

"Oh God," Jem whined. She sat next to Billy and put his head in her lap.

Kyle knelt by the bunk. There was blood everywhere. Billy's mouth opened, but Kyle couldn't make out any words.

"Billy, you're going to be fine," Jem said softly, brushing his dark hair out of his face. "Billy…Billy…"

165

Kyle thought the nerd's face looked like a mask, it was so ashen.

"I'm so sorry, Billy." Kyle couldn't think of anything else to say. He touched Billy's leg. A gesture of solidarity.

Billy blinked at him. A moment later his eyes stopped moving. His head fell limp in Jem's lap.

"Neal could be anywhere," Kyle whispered, an alien feeling, maybe grief, tugging at his insides.

"Right," Jem said, tears staining her cheeks as she disengaged from Billy's body.

Kyle heard a noise and grabbed Jem's hand.

"Get down!" he hissed.

They sprawled out on the floor, out of view of the windows.

"Did he see us?" Kyle whispered.

"I don't know."

Oh God, oh God, oh God.

Neal yelled again. Kyle guessed he was still on the path outside, somewhere between the office and the cabins. Hopefully, the deranged jock would keep on the paths, chasing after shadows. He imagined a wolf chasing its own tail and realized he'd much rather confront a wolf than Neal.

The seconds ticked by. Kyle's breathing started to slow down. He wiped sweat off his brow. Jem looked too afraid to move an inch. They lay on the floor facing each other, staring into each others' eyes.

He wanted to say something to Jem, to comfort her, but he couldn't risk making any noise. Neal could be right outside for all he knew. Kyle glanced up toward the windows, just waiting to see Neal's silhouette, but it didn't come.

He could sense Billy's body above them on the bed. The thought of the skinny nerd dead—killed by Neal—made him feel sick. A weird sort of guilt squirmed through him. He'd been horrible to Billy, and now Billy was dead.

The fight hadn't been against Billy. It never had been.

"If he comes in, are you ready to fight?" Jem whispered.

"I've never been in a fight before. There was one bully at school, but I just slept with him."

"If Neal comes in, we'll jump him together," Jem said, her voice barely audible.

"Okay."

Kyle visualized the front door bursting open and he and Jem rushing at Neal. They'd have to take the knife from him. Maybe with the scissor wound, and a lot of luck, the two of them could subdue him.

As Kyle stared into Jem's eyes through her messy purple hair, she suddenly convulsed. Her dark eyes bulged, and her head lifted up from the wooden floor. Kyle recoiled, drawing his lanky limbs up close to his shivering body.

Something silver flashed next to Jem's head. Kyle gasped. The knife had impaled her through the gaps in the floorboards. Kyle jumped off the floor and dove onto the nearest bunk bed.

Jem's head crashed back to the floor with a sickening thud, and Kyle heard the knife sliding back out of her.

He's under the cabin, but not for long.

Chapter 23

Kyle got to his feet and ran. He had to get as far away from Neal as possible. The irony of that fact wasn't lost on him. The guy he'd spent the past week mooning over and trying to get close to was now the one guy he needed to get far, far away from.

He heard scuffling sounds beneath the cabin.

"Stay the hell away from me!" he yelled as he ripped open the cabin door. He tore out into the night.

He had to find the others. Safety in numbers. There was no way he could take Neal on alone.

The rest of the campers couldn't be far away. Although he knew running into the forest was a stupid idea—he'd seen those movies—he had no choice. Town was too far and he doubted he'd be able to hitchhike at this time of night.

His only chance was finding the other campers.

They're dead. Jem. Billy. Cobb. Everyone.

He tried to swallow the thought. Bile burned the back of his throat at the memory of Jem alive and then suddenly not. The light had gone from her eyes and there was so much blood.

No way in hell is that happening to me.

Kyle pushed his body as hard as he could, out of the cabin and toward the kitchen. Donny was the only adult around. Kyle flung the screen door open and called out, "Donny! Donny, are you in here?"

He ran around the steaming pot of chili and found a red pool collecting on the floor. It didn't look like chili. He followed the source to one of the cabinets. He forced himself to open the door and found Donny's body stuffed inside, bent in a hideous pose.

Kyle slammed the door shut and spun around. *Where's Neal? He could be anywhere.*

He raced out of the kitchen and through the camp, heading for the lake. He could skirt around the edge and listen for the rest of the campers. That was preferable to entering the forest.

He slowed as he ran, spotting a vehicle through the underbrush. It looked like the kind of van Brady might buy when he got older.

Maybe it's a stoner!

Kyle hurried toward the van and quickly saw that something was wrong with it. The hood was wide open. He made his way toward the driver's side and found some guy in his twenties sitting perfectly still, his eyes shut.

"Hey, hey!" Kyle banged on the window, but the guy didn't wake up.

Kyle opened the door and the guy's body fell down to the ground at his feet. He saw the wound in his neck and had to cover his mouth to keep from screaming.

Nowhere's safe.

Kyle sprinted away from the van on his way through the woods. As the lake came into view, a dark expanse of water under the moon, he thought he heard a noise. Was it behind him? Had Neal caught up?

The Closet Man. The Closet Man is Neal.

He still couldn't believe it. He'd overheard Billy and Jem whispering about something happening at the camp. They wanted to know what happened to Tommy. Nobody ever suspected Neal, though, and who could blame them? Everybody was too busy drooling over him. The perfect jock. The perfect guy.

The images kept flashing before his eyes.

Katherine's hanging body. Billy on the bed. Jem dead on the floor.

It was his own special brand of torture, far worse than anything he'd been subjected to at Camp Genesis. He couldn't help feeling like this was just another one of the camp's games. A test to see how he'd react to the deaths of all of his fag friends.

"Now, wasn't that fun?" he imagined Father Oliver saying with a sickening grin. *"All your friends are going to die. And you'll be next, because we all know that homosexuality is a sin."*

"Fuck you, Father," Kyle said through gritted teeth. "Don't stop. Stop and die."

He hurried to the lake and spotted the boathouse.

The double doors were open. Kyle remembered that Billy and Jem had been assigned to clean it that afternoon. A few tools were still strewn about and Kyle surveyed them, trying to figure out which one would work as a weapon.

The axe. Obviously.

He seized it and whirled around.

He'd definitely heard something that time. He hurried into the boathouse, hiding behind one of the doors. He peeked through a hole in the wood. There was Neal, caught in the moonlight. A pale goliath.

"Damn," Kyle muttered. He could see every one of the muscles in Neal's torso. If Neal found him, that was it. Game over. He'd be as dead as the others.

Kyle retreated further into the shadows of the boathouse. He tried to be as quiet as possible. The only thing that calmed his nerves was gripping the axe tightly. He'd have to swing it hard if Neal came through the door. Come out fighting.

Bitch, you're going down. Turning on your own people? You deserve every inch of this axe.

The water in the boathouse was still. Kyle felt like he was in a crypt. A dingy, cobwebby crypt. He remembered what Katherine had said. Her son was killed here.

Why had he come into the boathouse?

You're an idiot, Kyle Majors.

Something dripped on his forehead. Kyle reached up and wiped at it, looked at his hand. He frowned. In the dark it looked almost red.

"What the—" he began, peering up into the roof of the boathouse. Fresh horror gripped him.

Dead eyes stared down at him.

Bodies were wrapped in fishnets. Horribly ashen-faced bodies. One of them was the caretaker. Toombs. The other was the kid; the mousy one. Tommy. They were bound up as if they'd been caught by a giant spider.

"No," Kyle gasped.

"You found the others."

Kyle tensed.

Neal stood in the doorway. He leaned casually against the doorframe, his face in shadow. His white teeth flashed.

"You stay the hell back," Kyle warned.

"Me?" Neal gave him an innocent look. "Thought you'd be happy to finally have me alone. I've seen your looks. You've wanted to get me alone all week."

"Don't flatter yourself," Kyle spat.

"Thought you liked bad boys, Kyle." Neal inspected his knife. "And, Kyle, I've been very, very bad."

"You killed them."

Neal looked at him. His eyes were dark and glittering. "They needed purifying. All of them."

"Purifying? What are you, some kind of killer hippie?"

"They were beyond saving in this life. They had to die. They were disgusting. Evil." His bare shoulders tensed with anger and his attractive features became ugly. "You, too. I'm glad you're the last of that group. You're the worst. Bragging about your conquests, unashamed of your filthy behavior."

Kyle's gut twinged. People had called him a slut for as long as he could remember. He'd heard it all before, but hearing Neal say it hurt even more. Kyle reminded himself that this wasn't the Neal he had lusted after.

Neal was nuts.

"I'm proud of who I am," he said, though he was more afraid than ever.

He's going to kill me, just like he killed the others.

"And that's why you're going to die." Neal looked around the boathouse. "It ends where it began," he said, though he didn't seem to be talking to Kyle anymore. "I saw them here, together. They were laughing and..." Neal trailed off. He looked down at the knife in his hand. "They seemed happy. Miles tried to fool around with me once. He came to the movie theater in town when his parents were setting up the camp. He kept looking at me before the movie started and then I went to the restroom and he followed... Then they were here together, their hands all over each other, laughing. My parents wanted me to come here and I just knew Katherine would close the camp if something happened to her slutty son. I found something sharp and they didn't laugh anymore..."

Without warning, he lunged at Kyle.

Kyle swung the axe, but Neal ducked and the weapon embedded itself in the wall.

Pain exploded in Kyle's jaw and he realized Neal had punched him. He fell back, nearly tripped over some rope, but caught himself just in time.

Neal raised the bloodied knife and brought it down.

Kyle threw both of his hands up and caught Neal's arm. He was so strong. Neal's weight bore down on him and it took all of Kyle's strength to keep that quivering blade from going straight into his chest.

His heart hammering, Kyle kicked Neal in the crotch with everything he had.

"Didn't you know? I fight dirty," he hissed as Neal sank to his knees. Kyle brought his knee up into Neal's nose, and he heard a sickly crunch.

As Neal struck the floor, Kyle leapt over him, going for the axe. Hands seize his legs suddenly, squeezing hard, and Kyle cried out as he toppled straight into the water.

It was surprisingly cold. Kyle barely had a chance to gasp a breath before he was submerged. Water rushed over his head.

It was so dark he couldn't see anything. Just indistinct shapes and bubbles bursting from his mouth.

He swept the water with his hands and attempted to break the surface, but something seized his head and held him under.

Panic surged through him. He needed air.

He struggled, flailing at the hand gripping him, but Neal refused to give in. Kyle stared up and saw Neal's face rippling through the water. He looked madder than ever.

Kyle thrashed and squirmed, attempting to free himself.

Neal had an iron grip and he couldn't escape it.

His chest felt like it was going to explode. He clamped his mouth shut and tried to stay calm. Perhaps if he stopped thrashing? Pretended he'd drowned?

Neal's never going to let go.

His chest burned and his mind screamed at him to draw a breath. If he opened his mouth, though, he'd suck in a lungful of dirty lake water and then it'd all be over.

He was going to drown.

Neal had won.

As the pain in his chest increased, everything became blurry. All he could feel was the iron grip and the cramping, desperate need to open his mouth.

Don't do it. Don't do it!

The world faded into a dark, soupy nightmare. He stopped thrashing. Tiredness washed through him. This was it. He couldn't think clearly anymore.

I can't believe this is it.

Kyle felt himself becoming resigned to his fate. He was floating.

He opened his mouth and water rushed inside.

Then, suddenly, there was nothing holding him under anymore. Something grabbed his shoulders and Kyle was dimly aware of being heaved up out of the water. He wasn't floating anymore. He was laid out on the floorboards.

Hands beat his chest and he spluttered, coughing water all over himself.

He gasped like a fish, drew in his first breath in what felt like forever. His chest cramped and contracted painfully.

"Kyle. Come on, Kyle."

Kyle looked up, his eyes adjusting to the dark of the boathouse.

Father Oliver peered down at him, worry lines creasing his face.

"Neal," Kyle choked.

"Come on," the priest urged, helping Kyle to his feet. He saw a body on the floor. Neal lying face down. The back of his head was bloody. A rusty bucket sat beside him.

"You..." Kyle said, leaning on Father Oliver. "He's a nutcase."

They reached the open double doors.

"H-he killed them," Kyle stammered, still dazed. Everything felt like a dream. "All of them."

"I know," Father Oliver said softly. "I know."

The priest cried out suddenly in surprise as he was wrenched away.

Barely able to stand without the support, Kyle turned and saw that Father Oliver was against the wall, held there by Neal.

"NO!" Kyle yelled. He felt weak with fear.

"You're all dead!" Neal bellowed, his hands wrapped around the priest's neck. Father Oliver beat at Neal, but there was no stopping him. The priest's eyes bulged and he choked, unable to get free.

As if in a dream, Kyle found there was suddenly a knife in his hand. He must have picked it up off the floor. Then he was behind Neal, and Neal yelled in pain. A high, angry yell.

Father Oliver collapsed, panting, to the floor.

Kyle saw that the knife was in Neal's back, between his shoulder blades. He'd put it there. The thought made him feel sick, but he knew he'd done it.

Neal had to be stopped.

Fresh panic seized him as Neal rounded on him. He grabbed Kyle's shoulders, eyes wide, blood dribbling from his mouth.

"Get off me!" Kyle cried, but Neal was so strong and they collapsed to the floor. His back struck the floorboards. Neal was on top of him. Kyle tried to push him off, but he was too heavy.

Neal's hands went for his neck.

"I'm all yours," Neal gurgled, fresh blood spilling down his chin.

"Fuck you," Kyle snapped. He reached up and grabbed the knife in Neal's back. He twisted and wrenched at it and Neal howled.

"You give gays a bad name," Kyle yelled, dragging the knife free.

"Fucking queer," Neal groaned.

"And you're a massive hypocrite," Kyle said. He buried the knife in Neal's throat. The other boy writhed against him. A torrent of blood erupted from his neck and Neal collapsed on top of him.

With a grunt, Kyle shoved him off.

Neal lay still.

"Can't believe I ever liked you," Kyle muttered. Father Oliver helped him to his feet again.

"Are you okay?"

Kyle looked at him and gathered his breath. He straightened and rearranged his T-shirt, ignoring the blood stains and the pain in his chest.

"Looks like I'll live."

● ● ●

Together, Kyle and Father Oliver returned to the camp in the near pitch dark.

"Time to get out of this dump," Kyle murmured.

"You're lucky to be alive," Father Oliver said.

"Thanks for that."

"It's a good thing I came back when I did," the priest breathed. "The others…they weren't so lucky."

After several minutes, they emerged out of the woods and into the camp proper. Kyle had never been so thankful to see the cluster of cabins in the moonlight.

As they passed the younger girls' cabin, the front door flew suddenly open.

Kyle nearly jumped out of his skin.

Then he saw who it was.

"Christ, don't do that," he told Steven.

The other boy wiped his bleary eyes. "Fell asleep cleaning," he lisped, his headphones still around his neck. "What I miss?"

Kyle just looked at him.

"What?" Steven asked.

"The others will be back in a few hours," Father Oliver said. "I need to call the police. You boys come with me now, please."

"Neal cut the line in Katherine's office," Kyle said.

"Let's see if my phone's working, then. It's temperamental

and I've had trouble getting through to people on it before, but I think we've had our share of bad luck tonight."

The boys followed Father Oliver to his cabin.

"What's going on?" Steven asked.

"I'll explain everything inside." Father Oliver opened the door and escorted Steven inside.

Lingering outside, Kyle surveyed the camp. This place was responsible for Neal. He'd gone crazy. The camp had turned him into a monster.

A hot monster.

Kyle looked at the archway over the camp entrance with its dull writing.

Camp Genesis.

Through the weariness, sudden anger spiked hotly. He reached down and picked up a large rock.

Tommy, Toombs, Brady, Cobb, Matthew, Michaela, Billy, Jem.

Neal.

Anger throbbing through him, he hurled the rock at the sign. It smashed a small hole in the rotten wood, sending wood chips to the ground.

Panting, Kyle resisted casting a look back at the camp, instead trudging down the dirt track, away from the carnage, toward the main road.

He ignored Steven's calls.

He'd hitch a ride to town, back to reality. Talk to the police there. Call his parents. There'd be reporters and sensational headlines. They'd call him the Gay Camp Massacre Survivor. They'd want to know everything about him.

Kyle felt tears sliding down his cheeks.

"Camp's dismissed," he muttered to himself.

Epilogue

Article from the Colorado Daily Times *dated July 21, 1986*

Gay camp massacre claims young victims
By CHRIS THOMPSON
Staff Writer

A remote summer camp in Lake County, Colorado was the scene of a series of brutal murders that claimed the lives of at least six teenagers.

Camp Genesis, run by 42-year-old Katherine Creevey, began its summer session on July 16, and ended in a bloodbath this week when a troubled camper went on a murderous rampage.

The camp is notorious as one of the country's controversial "gay camps" for teenagers struggling with their sexuality.

Among the victims were Mrs. Creevey and a number of teenage campers whose names have yet to be released to the press. The victims' families are being informed by the authorities.

"I'm just glad to be alive," said Kyle Majors, 18, one of the campers who survived the massacre. Talking exclusively to the Colorado Daily Times, Majors added: "I lost a lot of friends and I hold Camp Genesis fully responsible for their deaths. Homosexuality isn't some sickness to cure."

Although police haven't confirmed the exact number of victims, it appears that at least 11 people died at the camp.

The Colorado Daily Times is currently investigating claims that the camper responsible for the murders remains at large.

About the Authors

Elliot Arthur Cross is a New England author and avid horror fan. After college, he left the exciting world of retail behind to commit to writing. He has published several stories at JMS Books and its YA imprint QueerTeen Press. When he's not writing horror (or watching Netflix), Elliot works in other genres like mystery, adult, and the supernatural. For more on his solo projects, check out www.elliotarthurcross.com.

Joshua Winning is a film journalist and author of dark fantasy series The Sentinel Trilogy (available through Peridot Press). He is a contributing editor at Total Film magazine, and also writes for SFX and Digital Spy. He is co-founder of the Night Terrors book series, which launched in 2014 with gay murder mystery Camp Carnage and continues with 13 Tales To Give You Night Terrors. Joshua lives in North London and can be found online at www.joshuawinning.com and on Twitter @JoshWinning.

If you enjoyed this book, please consider leaving a positive review on major book review sites like Amazon, Smashwords and Goodreads. Reviews really do help spread the word and without them we wouldn't be able to keep doing what we love – writing the scariest things we can imagine for your delectation! Thanks for your support and we look forward to reading your reviews.

● ● ●

The **NIGHT TERRORS** anthology begins with

CAMP CARNAGE

and continues with

ELECTRIC SCREAMS

a supernatural tale of revenge

coming early 2016.

Made in United States
Orlando, FL
26 April 2025

60800640R00103